D1351761

RETURN

RUSTY

Born in one of the worst storms the North West Highlands of Scotland has ever known, orphaned by fire, savaged by beast and man, Rusty, the red deer calf, knew little of security.

Then one day he was rescued by Angus the gamekeeper and given to his daughter Jeannie to aid her recovery from a car crash in which her fiancé was killed.

This story vividly evokes the harsh but rewarding life of the Highlands, with both natural tragedies and those contrived by man's inadequacies, and with moments of peace and intense satisfaction.

As readers of her earlier books know, Joyce Stranger arouses equal interest in both human and animal characters. She is a trained scientist, writing without sentimentality and with strict adherence to fact, with a deep feeling for wild animals and tame, and for those who are involved with them.

'Fascinating reading. There are many delightful descriptions of wild life in the Highlands, its daily drama and unceasing activity.'   *Huddersfield Examiner*

'I wept, as I wept when I first read *White Fang* and *Black Beauty*. The background is superbly done.'
                     Wendy Monk, *Birmingham Post*

VAL'S READ 'N' RETURN

Also by Joyce Stranger

and published by Corgi Books

Joyce Stranger

Rusty

CORGI BOOKS
A DIVISION OF TRANSWORLD PUBLISHERS LTD

RUSTY

A CORGI BOOK 0 552 08633 9

Originally published in Great Britain
by Harvill Press Ltd.

PRINTING HISTORY
Harvill Press edition published 1969
Corgi edition published 1971
Corgi edition reprinted 1973
Corgi edition reissued 1976
Corgi edition reprinted 1977
Corgi edition reprinted 1979
Corgi edition reprinted 1982

Copyright © Joyce Stranger Limited 1969

Conditions of sale
1: This book is sold subject to the condition that it
shall not, by way of trade *or otherwise*, be lent, re-sold,
hired out or otherwise *circulated* without the publisher's
prior consent in any form of binding or cover other than
that in which it is published *and without a similar
condition including this condition being imposed on
the subsequent purchaser.*
2: This book is sold subject to the Standard Conditions
of Sale of Net Books and may not be re-sold in the U.K.
below the net price fixed by the publishers for the book.

This book is set in 10/11 pt Plantin

Corgi Books are published by Transworld Publishers Ltd.,
Century House, 61-63 Uxbridge Road,
Ealing, London W5 5SA.
Made and printed in Great Britain by
Hunt Barnard Printing Ltd., Aylesbury, Bucks.

To Lilian Daykin,
who gives me constant encouragement,
with my love

To Cliff Dallas,
who guessed it right, and who insisted
on explaining it.

All people, events and places
in this book are fictitious.

Rusty

Chapter One

All the demons in hell were loose on the mountain the night that Rusty was born. The red deer hid, terrified.

The hind herd had taken shelter in a corrie, halfway up the steep pine-clad slopes of the Dragon, the monster hill that shadowed the Nine Glens. Here they tried, in vain, to find protection from rain that was driven by howling fiends that rode on the wind, screaming through the trees, bowing and bending the swaying branches in a dervish dance of insanity. Thunder bounded from the peaks, echoing, rumbling, the drum-rolls alarming not only the hinds on the lower slopes, but the antlerless stags that haunted the steeper parts of the mountain.

The cowering beasts listened, ears moving, now forward, now back, catching the echo that came from north, from south, from east, from west, that pealed up the slope and down the hill, as if all the world had gone mad. A tree swayed from its roots and fell with a tearing crash. The herd shifted, moving fearfully, led by the old hind, the great-great-grandmother of the youngest beast, wise with age, grey with years, wary with the skill she had gathered so hardily in her long and eventful life.

Even she had never known a storm like this. She watched uneasily as lightning flashed and flamed and flared across the sky, forking ripples over the peaks, cleaving the clouds and the shadowed night that brought such unusual clamour.

Rain filled the tiny streams that gushed from the rocky runnels, waterfalls surged in churning uproar, and the burn brimmed to race in spate, clattering boulders and flinging them over the banks. That was a new hazard, a hazard that brought the young otter family helter-skelter from their bankside holt, to crouch under drenched bracken and shiver with cold and fright.

Rusty's mother was very close to her time. Terror brought her to term, so that the calf dropped in thick clumped heather, and lifted his small head and stared in shocked bewilderment at the strange place that was giving him so noisy and so chilly a welcome.

The hind was young, and this was her first calf, but her instincts were strong and she had seen other hinds give birth before. She moved her body, so that she took the worst of the wind and rain upon herself. The baby crouched beside her, staring intently at the sky that split so mystifyingly to reveal arched flashes of multi-coloured light that dazzled him and forced him to close half-blinded eyes against the glare.

His mother was warm, and her tongue comforted him, licking away the covering of birth. She was unable to keep him dry or more than partly sheltered. The old hind, aware of the event, nosed her way into the bracken cover, welcomed the calf with her own red tongue, and then settled against him, so that both bodies shielded him. Another hind stood guard, ears pricked, eyes wary, head turning, ready to stamp at the first hint of trouble, ready to alert the herd to instant flight.

Nothing stirred in the night. Men, who brought the greatest danger, carrying it in weapons that spat noise and flame and death, were all at home and abed. The fox and the vixen had hunted swiftly and briefly and returned to lie with their cubs, and tremble at the stupendous volume of sound that roared above the mountain. The wild cat hid with her kits and trembled too.

By the time that Rusty was eight hours old the storm had blown itself out. The sun, watery and fickle, flamed briefly above the Nine Glens, and then, as the clouds shifted, poured welcome warmth, causing the sodden ground to steam mistily, surprising the little calf even more, as he watched moving tendrils coil and swirl across his small body, and tried to nose them,

12

to feel them, expecting solid matter and finding only a wet mystery that swathed the nearby trees and hid them from him. His mother had left him alone by now, safely hidden in dense cover. She did not return until he was twelve hours old.

He staggered to his feet and found his food, and the hind licked him, avidly aware of him, of his new life, of his small mouth thrusting and tugging, of his busy tail wagging appreciation as he drank. When he had finished she licked his milky face, and nosed him sharply into the bracken, where he crouched like a dead creature, already knowing his first lesson.

She left him as she grazed, but returned often, each time meeting his upturned muzzle with a swift affectionate lick, each time reinforcing her command with a nose that thrust him into cover, that hid him from scavenging fox and prowling wild cat and questing eagle, that ensured his safety for another day. He was very small, and even a marauding dog could end his brief life.

Rusty knew that he must not move, but he did not mind. He slept, and gained strength. He fed, and learned very soon to watch for his mother coming back to him, to answer her faint bark of enquiry with his own pleased bleat, to know her smell, and to recognise it among the scents of the other hinds, who often came near, and also of the old one, the great-great-grandmother, who watched over him too, baby-sitting when his mother was grazing far away, ensuring safety for all those within her care.

She had been barren now for three years, and Angus McLeod, the keeper, sometimes wondered if he should cull her. But she was so wary that no one could come within firing distance of the hind herd and he decided to leave her. She would keep the deer safe, and there were too many trigger-happy youths from the cities, out in a van for a day's fun, ready to blaze off at any animal, leaving it, often, to roam with a a festering wound that slowly weakened it, leaving the keeper to track down the beast and deal his own swift mercy.

From his cover of bracken Rusty watched the world about him. If he looked up, he saw bare slate-blue peaks towering into the sky, and his eyes also noted the great stags moving across the slopes, climbing high, away from the hind herd, anxious to regrow their antlers, and live alone through the uneasy months when each head throbbed and ached with new-growing horn, and the hot velvet was sore and painful to any touch, so that a branch snapped back across a budding antler was sharp torment, and heads were held with care.

Below the tree line the massed pines spiked towards the clouds. Rusty watched the tops move in the wind, looking up through needled, shivering leaves. Sometimes he looked skywards, mystified by the scudding clouds and the birds that swooped and dived and rode on the thermals, gliding in easy movements that were freer even than the long loping bounds of the running deer.

Close to him was thymy turf and spiky prickling heather; bracken that was almost always wet with rain; small petalled yellow saxifrages, and stunted shrubby bushes back-combed by the never-ceasing wind that rode the mountain. Below him the ground slipped away, tree-clad, to the loch, where waves tumbled endlessly in a smother of creaming foam, and the two-legged beasts that lived in the strange places at the foot of the hill went about their intriguing operations. He knew nothing of man save that he was dangerous, and that when man came near the herd ran from him, the calves racing with their dams, panic fear forcing them to melt into cover, where they hid and watched, eyes wide, ears listening, and sniffed the fouled air, and waited until the taint had gone from the heather.

Rusty could not guess that his life was soon to be bound with that of the men he so feared. He learned his lessons well. He fled from the human smell that lingered on the ground where man had walked, he bolted from their prowling, barking dogs that tried to pull down the weaker hinds. He hid, trembling, when an illicit gun blazed out on the flank of the Dragon, and watched, from a safe distance, his mother beside him, the other hinds nearby, as the keeper came with his dog, and yelled in fury at the poacher.

14

Chapter Two

Angus McLeod had been keeper for longer than he cared to remember. He knew every inch of the Nine Glens, knew the wicked moods of weather that could scour and rake the Dragon, knew every beast in the deer herd and every sheep on the hill.

He was a tall man, big-boned, with red hair now turning grey, with a quiet way with him that beasts trusted, and a gentleness that extended only to animals. He had a rare impatience with people, finding them often irritating, and frequently cruel.

He was a quiet man, but his tongue could be bitter, and there were several men in the Nine Glens who could testify to this. He had blazed in fury at Donald McCann, who was one of the foresters, for whipping a tired pony; had blistered with his tongue two of the hotelkeeper's sons who had shot and injured a hind at the far end of the Nine Glens and left her to drag a wounded leg until he found her blood trail and shot her to save her further agony.

Men respected Angus, but only those who knew him well really liked him. Others thought him stern and dour and ill-tempered not realising that his passion for living creatures made him shout his wrath at those who caused pain to beasts that had done them no harm and that were defenceless.

His wife was dead, and for over three years he had lived by himself in the stone house that crouched under the trees halfway up the Dragon. It was a lonely place, looking down through the pines to the loch far beneath, to the loch that was blue in summer when the sun shone bright, and grey in winter, and was always edged with brilliant orange wrack, and traced with a drift of foam that frothed and feathered the rocky margin.

He was no longer alone. His daughter had come back to Scotland, and now, as he walked on the hill, watching for lambs that had ventured unwisely, noting the nests of grouse and capercaillie, watching for newcomers among the calves that ran with the hinds, he sighed. Life had not been easy since Jeannie came home.

It seemed only a short time since she had left, full of laughter and plans, and gone to London. Her letters had been eager, telling of her work, nursing in a big hospital, which she loved, and later, of the man she had met and whom she would soon marry.

She had come home for a brief visit, bringing Robert with her, and Angus had liked him at sight and found him easy to talk with and interested in the wild life on the hill, a way of living that was new to him. He had been born and bred in a town. They should have married two months ago.

Instead, Jeannie was home, limping from injuries sustained when a crook in a getaway car had rammed Robert's vehicle. Robert was buried in his home village, and Jeannie cared for nothing and nobody. She rarely spoke. She kept the house clean and cooked the meals, and for the rest of the day sat and watched the wind sweep through the trees and fling high the waters of the loch.

She could not help it, poor lass, Angus thought, and sighed. He did not want to go back into the little house where time hung endlessly, and every word he spoke seemed to echo in an empty room. If only he could capture her interest. She was not yet twenty-one, and should be reaching out to the world again. She would be better away. Or would she? Angus did not know. He only knew that he could do nothing for her, that no word of his would comfort her, that it was worse to sit back and watch her pain than to bear his own, and that she had made his life more empty instead of filling it, for now he

16

missed his wife even more. She might have known how to cope.

He sat, sucking the stem of an empty pipe. He did not smoke, although he enjoyed tobacco, because he knew that the rank scent frightened away the beasts, and he liked to watch them, to stalk them, to come upon them and see them close. The harbouring stag, the wary hind, her calf at foot, the blue hare crouching, his nose reading the wind. Each sighting was a triumph.

It was a lonely world, too lonely for a girl, high up on the Dragon. The nearest house was in the fifth of the Nine Glens, where the unmarried foresters lived. The village, on the far side of the loch, was a half day away, and the only town of any size too far for a day's journey. It was not right that Jeannie should be marooned. She needed people. But he could not make her go, nor did he even dare to hint it, lest she felt unwelcome.

He sighed again. It was time to go home. His supper would be ready, and that in itself was a penance, for Jeannie had no interest in cooking, and the food was wretched. He could make better meals himself, but did not dare suggest that he tried. He was on a tightrope, and every step needed thought and care.

The grey pony was waiting patiently for supper. He petted him, and Grey nuzzled Angus's head and then turned to the manger where his feed awaited him. There had been rats gnawing the corner of one of the sacks. Angus fetched the old Tom and locked him in for the night. The cat nosed the corner of the stall, and sat patiently, knowing well why he was there. Bartie, the second pony, stamped irritably, demanding his own share, stabled behind the cottage.

Jeannie had fed the chickens and locked them in. Angus checked the fastenings and checked the wooden walls. There were too many hill foxes and they were bold with hunger, having cubs to feed. Twice he had sent a charge of shot after a fleeing shape in the moonlight.

'There's a new calf on the hill. Born in the storm, perhaps,' he said, easing his long legs under the table.

Jeannie nodded. Once she would have gone to look, but now nothing mattered. Life stretched emptily in front of her, and memory was bitter. Robert had gone walking up the hill, only last year, to see another calf born there, and she had gone with him, and they had laughed and talked. . . . She pushed away her plate and went outside and sat on the wall, looking down at the wind-racked waters, listening to the plangent moan of the sobbing trees. Rain drifted on the air, but she did not feel it, nor did she feel the chill that crept up the hillside. The grey sky and the grey water echoed her mood.

Inside the cottage Angus finished his meal and washed the dishes. Useless to go and coax her in. He sat at the table and entered the day's events in his notebook; the finding of a nest of grouse chicks at the far edge of the moor, the new calf in the hind herd, the reappearance of the Hill Master, a giant stag that had vanished in the rutting season, and cantered up the hill that morning. He was now lurking in his old haunt above the peathag where he often wallowed when the Rut dominated the beasts, masking his gleaming chestnut coat with black and stinking mud.

The two pointers lay curled against one another. Tess's eyes were open, watching her master, but Mac slept soundly, and dreamed of rabbits, his hind leg thumping the rug, his tail beating softly and absurdly. Angus put out a booted foot and rubbed the dog's back and the tail accelerated momentarily and twitched, and then was still. The collies lay on the far side of the rug, exhausted. A log slipped in the hearth and Angus turned his head as he heard his daughter's footsteps on the stone flags of the little hall, and then the lig-lag sound as she limped forlornly up the stairs to her room, and the decisive slam of the door. He sat for a long time, watching the fire blaze and die and fall in a heap of lifeless ash, and had not the energy to stir himself and make a drink and bolt the door and go to bed.

Sleep was useless. He could not lie another night and watch the moon cast shadows on the walls and hear soft sobs from the other room. He took his gun and whistled his pointers and went out into the dark.

There was a ghost of a moon, high and thin, a pale slit in the sky. Its faint luminescence cast a glow through the trees, and far below, on the other side of the invisible water, the yellow lamps of the village spanned the single street and straggled up the hill, and a solitary car, easing its way slowly along the road that bordered the loch, swathed the sky with twin headlights.

The pointers came at heel, both silent, ready to drop at a whispered word. Angus trod softly, down through the garden where stunted shadowy bushes huddled against the ground, and out on to the path that the sheep used when they climbed the higher slopes of the Dragon.

Underfoot the ground was soft with needles from the pines. An owl called broodingly, a mouse rustled in the bushes, startling both pointers to attention. Angus's whispered command brought their tails to half mast but they obeyed him without hesitation.

Under the trees the shadows were thick and here Angus waited, leaning against a trunk that protected him from the wind. The wind blew from the loch, blew up and over the Dragon, scythed down the Nine Glens, and sang in the branches so that there was a constant rustling and murmuring that was echoed on every side.

Darkness blackened Jeannie's room. Far below lights began to flicker and die in the village, one by one, until at last only the evenly spaced street lamps indicated that there were men and houses and occupations over there. A riding light showed where a boat lay at anchor, moving lazily as the lapping waves rocked her hull.

There were eyes in the darkness. Angus watched, distinguishing the dark shape of a shoulder, the curve of the head, and the growing antlers, still in velvet, not yet flaunting the pride of maleness that ennobled the stags in the autumn roaring. Then the hill was bedevilled with wind and alive with excitement and the beasts vied for supremacy and stole hinds

19

for their own harem, and challenged each other with upraised voice and clashing antlers, and a wild urgency savaged the Dragon and spread through the Nine Glens and mastered the beasts.

Angus saw the shadowy stag turn his head. The wind had veered. It blew across the Dragon, warning the beast of man, and within seconds he had gone, fading noiselessly, effortlessly, blending into darkness, leaving behind him nothing but a memory of power.

It was quiet on the hill. Only the wind moved. No sign of man, or beast, no threat of danger. A deep sighing that came from a ewe suckling her lamb, a call from a lamb that was lost, and a swift gruff answer. A huff from a stirring pony in the silent stable, and the scuffle of the Tom cat pouncing. A cold nose sought Angus's hand. It was late and long past bedtime, and the dogs were tired.

He looked at the sky. The moon was draped in rags, and the shredded clouds were silver beneath her. A star shone above the loch and another glittered above him. It was cold in the chilly dark.

Angus shivered and went indoors. He locked and bolted his home, ordered the dogs on guard at the foot of the stairs and went to his room. There was no sound from Jeannie.

His pillow was hard. He thumped it despairingly, and stared out of the narrow window at the sky. The clouds were building over the loch, and the wind was rising. Tomorrow a gale would bluster from the west, and the little boat would toss uneasily in its berth, and the wind would howl again in the trees, and there would be more rain. And that would bring new worries.

Chapter Three

The wild cat had her lair under a tumbled cairn of rocks beyond the burn that fed into the stream at the top of the first of the Nine Glens. She had five mewing kits that savaged her for milk, and her mate brought food that barely satisfied her own ravening need.

He brought small rabbits and mice and birds, having eaten his fill as he hunted. She, as soon as the kits were old enough to leave, found food for herself, but there was never enough. Not enough for six bodies to fatten, or six mouths to feed.

Both cats were vigilant. The eagle had young in his own nest and often could be seen gliding above them, his sharp eyes watching for movement that would bring a reward for the hungry ever-open mouths in the eyrie on the high crag that topped the Dragon. Wild cat kittens were young and tender and easy prey when only a few days old.

He brought home rabbit and mountain hare, and a lamb dead at birth and left unburied by the shepherd in the fourth of the Nine Glens who knew it would soon be gone. Angus never left lambs on his side of the hill if he could avoid it. A taste for lamb might result in an ailing beast attacked, and not a dead one carried away. And stillborn lambs fed the dogs and saved his meagre purse.

The foxes were ravenous too. It had been a hard winter and many of the smaller creatures had died of cold and hunger.

Fear stalked daily, crept over the heather on the Dragon, marched in bold daylight in the secret depths of the Nine Glens, and startled the stags on the high hills, so that none ever

21

relaxed. Even when the herd was resting the watchers kept vigil, ready to stamp or bark at terror, ready to call the beasts to their feet, ready to run.

The crunch of a foot on rock, the snap of a twig, a taint on the wind, and, in a moment, where there had been many deer feeding, there was nothing. Only a memory of shapes that flitted into cover, the soft sound of a calf bleating its agitation, the sight of the vanishing herd, and a silence that was all the greater because it was unnatural.

The vixen could not get within yards of the hinds, nor could the dog fox, and the hovering eagle knew better than to test the maternal fury that would be unleashed should he attempt to add deer calf to his menu. Only the wild cats saw the calves, and slavered. Here was wealth.

It was snow that betrayed them.

Weather on the Dragon was always unpredictable, but not even Angus remembered snow in late June. It came in the night, stealthily, white feather flakes hiding rock and heather, masking the sides and roots of trees and clinging to brambles. When morning came the sun shone and the snow glittered smooth and hid gully and rill and runnel and the deer were dark unhappy shapes revealed for all to see.

Angus, busy with the dogs, digging out sheep and lambs that had been trapped, was conscious of them, of the uneasiness that kept them moving, pawing away the cold and clammy covering in search of food. The calves were, at first, bewildered and then found pleasure in frolicking, running in the shallower patches, nosing down through the snow and shaking small heads to free them from the unfamiliar substance that both chilled and puzzled them.

The wild cats had separated. The female had not fed well for two days, and hunger was riding her. The kits had drained her dry. Soon they would be weaned and then even more food would be needed. She stalked down the Dragon, the wind caressing her from nose tip to tail tip, belly close to the ground, ears flat on her head, eyes glowing. Her mouth was open in a silent snarl of anticipation.

22

Below her the old hind watched. There was no sound on the wind, no scent on the wind, but there was the taint of terror all around her. She had seen many snows fall and mask the Dragon and the Nine Glens, and she knew that when the drifts lay deep there was no sharp telltale footfall, and that she needed all her wits about her. The other beasts echoed her uneasiness. Heads lifted, ears moved constantly, never still, trying to gather sound from the silence, trying to outwit the many deaths that lay waiting for the unwary.

The wild cat was terror incarnate. She was wickedness walking on four tabby legs. She crept down the gullies, taking advantage of every hummock and tump, of every tiny knoll that would mask her presence. The wind stroked her softly from nose tip to tail tip. Once the deer saw her she was as conspicuous as they, and the final trial would lie in speed.

She caught the scent of the herd, the rich intoxicating deer tang, and her body ached for warm flesh and dripping blood, for the tear of teeth and slash of claw, for the moment of the kill, and the hours succeeding it. She would feed from plenty, ripping and gouging and feel her dry paps fill with milk and return to her lair, sated and fulfilled, and lie and purr with her kittens tugging at her, gathering vigour. Saliva poured from her mouth and she growled softly and menacingly to herself, unable to control her excitement.

The old hind heard the sound. Her ears lifted, her head turned, but the cat had crouched and was once more invisible, hidden behind a hummock, knowing that her eagerness must have betrayed her. She swallowed and swallowed again, too close now to show patience, as the full force of the deer tang bathed her senses, causing hunger to tempt her to insanity.

She leaped to the top of a knoll and looked at the herd, tail lashing, mouth wide, teeth gleaming, and she saw Rusty below her, and spat and sprang.

He caught her scent as she hurled herself towards him, and did not know what to do. No use cowering in snow. No cover anywhere. He leaped out of range and bleated his fear, and then the wild cat was above him, fur ruffled, enormity magnified, murder armed with tooth and claw, viciousness embodied. Panic seized him and his bleat sounded again, and the old hind heard him and turned and saw the wild cat and barked in anger.

A moment later Rusty's mother was beside him and her hard hooves caught the cat in the ribs and flung her sideways. The cat, hunger obsessing her, snarled and spat and a vicious paw raked the hind's flank and the scent of blood added new zest to the desire for food. The cat licked away saliva that crawled down her jaws, and twisted, her eyes on the calf. The hind was too large, even for her.

Rusty was unable to move. He had never dreamed of such horror. He was drowned in the rank stench that came from the brute, terrified by the full throated growl that she flung towards him, appalled by the flattened ears, the enormous lambent eyes, the wicked tongue curled backwards in the scarlet jaws, the vicious pointed fangs, the bristling whiskers, and the fluffed fur that enlarged the cat to more than normal size, so that it was a nightmare beast, the epitome of panic, the ultimate realisation of all unseen and half-feared horrors. He stood, unable to move his trembling legs, and watched the menace that sped towards him.

A second hind was level with them and her hooves shot out and the cat was once more flung sideways and then all the hinds were upon her, and the frightened calf watched, shaking, as hoof after hoof struck the now defenceless body, bringing crippling punishment and the beast tried to crawl away, her hunger forgotten in the shock of pain that racked her from the bruises and cuts and gashes that marred her splendid fur, in the realisation that she was helpless, that the deer had mastered her.

Until at last there was nothing left but darkness, and the pain had gone for ever, and the hinds, anxious to ensure safety for the calves, stamped and pounded her dying body, and made sure that their enemy was impotent.

The deer vanished and left the Tom cat widowed and the kittens motherless. A few days later the eagle made his kill.

And when Angus walked up the hill in the afternoon to look over the ground with the dogs to ensure that none of his sheep was trapped, there was nothing left but a stain of blood and mangled fur that marred the trampled snow.

Chapter Four

The snow vanished. Summer followed, unbelievable, swiftly on its heels, so that new green shoots were bright on the heather and harebells nodded under grey rocks, and boggy patches were starred with asphodel.

There was little rain, and for once Angus's ever-present fear of floods vanished, and he enjoyed the sunshine and the growing crops of chicks and calves and lambs, each day bringing new youngsters to increase the last year's stock.

The ground was dry and the brushy undergrowth in the forest became brittle and the ever present tangle of sticks under the trees made excellent kindling. Angus took an armful home with him every time he walked among the trees.

He was out all day and half the night, anxious that no poacher should trouble the herd. His spyglass swept the mountain, noting the moving stags, and the eagle watching for telltale of mouse or rat or young rabbit below him.

One morning in early July he found a lamb marooned on a rocky patch in the river. It had jumped the gap across the stream but could not jump back again, as this time it had to leap to the top of a high rocky bank. Angus climbed down and rescued it, and failed to see the old van that staggered up the forestry road into the woods, and parked in a clearing so that the occupants could camp for the night.

It did not occur to them that they were trespassing, or that they should ask permission to erect their tent. They had seen notices warning travellers of fire hazards, but had ignored them.

26

This was their first expedition. No one had ever taught them how to build a fire safely, or told them the most elementary rules of camping. They scattered their possessions on the grass, leaving the tent deserted while they sought huge bundles of firewood, which they stacked beside the van. In their absence one of the long legged rangy hill foxes found their parcel of frying steak, and made off with the unexpected bounty.

They stamped the grass flat and built their fire, and cooked bacon and egg and sausage, and sat by the blaze, laughing and talking. There were four of them, lads from Glasgow, who had saved for months to buy the van and tent and had come away from home for a brief taste of freedom.

It was good to be alone, without nagging parents, or bullying foremen to order them to work. It was good to be in the open, without restrictions of any kind on their behaviour. They swam under the waterfall, washed their shirts and socks in the burn that fed Angus's well, scared off every beast within a mile, and then, as dusk shadowed the Dragon and masked the Nine Glens, lay by the fire smoking and talking and drinking canned beer until they were too fuddled to think. They crept into their sleeping-bags, having made so fierce a blaze that the glare lit the mountain and alerted Andrew McKenzie, one of the foresters, who woke at two in the morning and, seeing it, took his Land-Rover and drove helter-skelter, frantic to find out what was causing the glow in the sky.

He was still on his way when one of the boys woke to the stink of burning cloth. It was almost dawn and the night's vagrant breeze had strengthened to blustery force. Wind fanned the piled branches to brilliant flame, and showered sparks that fell on the tent and dropped on the van and drifted on to the stacked brushwood. The lads, emerging sleepily into the rising sun, stared, as long flickering trickles of light crept through hay-high grass blades at the edge of the clearing and leaped into the trees, and the branches flared to startling life.

Andrew McKenzie, the forester, bucketing over the rough road that led to the clearing, swore as he saw black smoke and reddened flames spread skywards, where a dead tree had taken

27

light. He could now see the spreading line of hungry red, licking tongues devouring greedily, as they sped avidly over dry grass and bilberry and tussocky sere stems of last year's heather.

The four youths, staring at the inferno that surrounded them, panicked. They ran to the van, but the stack of stored brushwood was now also alight, burning so fiercely that they could not get near the vehicle. The tent, too, was ablaze, and they left everything, running pell-mell through the trees, choking and coughing as acrid smoke billowed about them and filled their lungs and tore at their eyes and seared their throats.

There had never been terror like this, not even in the drunken gang fights that broke out on Saturday evenings, not even when the other lads used flick knives, and steel-tipped boots, and razors. Then at least there was a chance of escape, but now everything was burning around them, and their fear increased as the petrol in the van's tank exploded with a roar and burning fabric was flung widespread, so that more trees and more grass fell victim to the greedy thrusting fire.

One of them, more intelligent than the other three, jumped into the burn, soaking himself, and battled his way downstream, staggering over rounded boulders, the surging current, moving faster than he, tearing at his legs, threatening to thrust him off his feet. His companions followed him.

Andrew McKenzie saw the blaze spreading, saw the tongues of flame lick skyward, saw smoke billow and roll, and turned his Land-Rover and rocketed back to the end of the road, arriving just as Angus wakened and stared in horror at the inferno devouring the Dragon.

He ran to the telephone and alerted the foresters, asked the village to send immediate help and yelled to Jeannie, who, for the first time since she had returned home, came running, shaken by the anger in her father's voice, her lagleg dragging less than usual.

He pointed to the mountain. She turned and gasped.

Andrew McKenzie put his head in at the door.

'The wind will keep it away from you. So long as it does

28

not change. Send the men to help me cut a fire break. I'll be on the first slope of the Dragon.'

He was away, leaving Angus to think the mountain well named, and to help Jeannie take the ponies out of the stable, and watch her set off down the hill. Grey was quiet, but little Bartie, nervous, being more highly bred, capered and shied and danced, so that Jeannie had to force him at every step. The smoke that stung his eyes worried him, and he tossed his head constantly. She wanted to reach the loch, where the farmer at Corrie Beg would put the ponies with his own beasts. They were safe enough there.

Angus whistled to the pointers and collies and strode up the flank of the Dragon. The sheep were racing, smoke driving them, and he sent the dogs to herd them, and reduce the flock to some semblance of order. He would have to hurry them and harry them.

The alternative was unthinkable. If fire caught those fleeces—Angus swallowed, sickened, and called to the dogs again. His shrill whistles guided them, now behind the sheep, now to the sides as they broke away, and now sounding behind them again. Tess to the left, over to the right, Mac behind her, both of them as able to herd as the wise old collie Star, who was running without instruction, preventing stragglers from breaking away, completely reliable, using his considerable brains, born to his work. The second sheepdog, Fly, was beside her master, ready to head off any beast that fled past.

The lambs added to the turmoil. They lost their mothers and ran back through the speeding flock, bleating, and the ewes pushed and thrust to reach them, answering them, so that the Dragon was hideous with noise, and the dogs had difficulty in hearing instructions.

Another barrage of whistles, and the beasts were lower on the hillside, but the drifting acrid smoke maddened them, and there was no chance to relax, no possibility of easing the pace or letting the sheep rest. The wind that scoured the slopes was fanning the flames, was spreading them through the forest, was flicking sparks over the heather, so that new foci flashed to brilliance, and there was no likelihood of the men stopping the conflagration. They could only widen the firebreaks and pray for rain, and there had been no rain for days.

Villagers were running up the hill. They nodded briefly to Angus and hurried on, cursing. There was work to do in the farms and the shops and crofts round the village, but that would have to wait. This threatened all of them. If the wind changed the fire might flash in an instant to the lower slopes of the Dragon, might cross the loch end, flaming among the trees that sheltered the caravan site, might spread to the boat-yard, stacked high with timber, and then to the garage where gallons of petrol had just been delivered into the vast under-ground tank, and the village would vanish in a holocaust. No time to lose.

No time to lose. Men moved cars and vans and lorries, men took boats out into the loch and left them wherever an anchor would find bottom, and rowed back in the dinghies and raced to help. The fire engines came roaring in, sirens screaming, and the women soaked their window curtains and hung them against the wood, and watched the smoke that hid the sun.

No time to lose. Angus chivvied the dogs and the dogs worked their hardest, and the seething mass of sheep covered the mountain slope. There were other sheep there now. Sheep branded with John McLeod's broad blue 'M', and with the red 'H' of the Hinton farm, and with the splashed purple crescent of Corrie Beg.

There were other creatures coming down the slope. A bird flew out of the trees, feathers blazing, and died in a scream of agony. Angus's Tom cat, ears flattened, tail bushed and erect, came flying past the moving flock, making automatically for lower ground near the loch. He did not even stop to greet the dogs as he ran.

The farmer from Corrie Beg met him, his own dogs at heel. 'I'll take them into my big field. Have to sort them later,' he said, and whistled his collies. Angus left Fly and Star with him and sent the pointers to guard the two ponies, and spoke briefly with Jeannie, who had gone back to the cottage and come to meet him with two rifles.

'I'm as good a shot as you,' she said, and Angus did not argue. It was true, and guns would be needed up there on the slope.

Men, faces black with smoke, reeking of burning wood, drenched in sweat, hacked and hewed at trees that were reluctant to die. The crash of trunks echoed among the roar and hiss and sigh of the flames, and the whole of the Dragon was etched, black and red and yellow, against the sulphur sky, and fiery trails spread from the main blaze like the fingers of a hand.

No one saw the four youths creep, soaking wet, from the burn, and slip away. There would be hell to pay if they were caught, but they never stayed to answer for any of their crimes. They had lost their van and their tent and their possessions, and the lesson would remain. No one was going to catch them.

There was water in the pool under the fall and the hoses drank it greedily and soaked the ground all round Angus's cottage, and soaked the carefully dried hay and the stables and the shed. It would take a long time to dry out again, but better than losing the lot.

A hare, maddened by pain and fear, ears flattened, eyes bolting from its skull, came flying past Jeannie, close enough to touch. The dark fur was singed black. The gun brought quick release, and then, looking at the beast, she found her throat closed and her eyes clouding with tears. She shook them away. There would be more creatures in torment, up there on the hill. No room for pity. She must harden herself.

The stags had been browsing above the flames and had taken refuge in the fifth of the Nine Glens. Foresters cutting the trees away to make a break on that side of the hill saw the leaping brown bodies sail gracefully past as they fled from horror.

The hinds had not been so lucky. Part of the herd had climbed, but half of them had been caught by fire, and broken through the ring of flame, and came running, blinded by smoke. Those that were badly hurt were quickly despatched, but some were left, as there seemed little more than fright wrong with

31

them. Small burns would heal and the herd would be sadly decimated so better not slaughter indiscriminately.

The wild cat came flying from the wood, his tail blazing. Angus shot him, and he died with a snarl of fury on his lips and all his claws extended in one last furious raking movement as he attempted to deal death to those who had so cruelly abused him. His tabby body was immense.

A forestry pony, marooned in the wood, came stampeding towards them, eyes rolling, body blackened and burnt. Jeannie was closest and the terrified beast was charging straight for her father, and she aimed and fired and killed and then fired again as a hind, scorched and shrieking, fled after him.

'It's a charnel house,' Angus said, savage anger riding him, delaying and preventing pity.

Andrew McKenzie came wearily towards them, almost un-recognisable. Tears running from smarting eyes had channelled his dirty face. A branch had fallen across his shoulder, burning both shirt and neck. Pain had forced him to give up fighting the fire.

Jeannie took one look at him and took him indoors. She and Andrew had sat next to each other in the school house, where children of all ages worked in one room, had played truant together, guddling the basking trout, had fought and made up and fought again. He had met Robert, and been sorry that Jeannie had set her mind elsewhere but perhaps now he could hope and he almost welcomed the pain that made her gentle towards him as she dressed the burn and bandaged it. She began to brew quarts of coffee, so that anyone stopping for a much-needed rest, or for attention because of injury, could have a drink too. She began to make sandwiches.

'You can keep away from the fire,' she said. 'If a spark falls on that bandage . . .'

'I'll drive down and fetch more bread,' Andrew answered. 'The men will need food.'

Jeannie glanced up at the Dragon, all apathy forgotten. The intense suffering of the beasts, and the danger to the men, had momentarily shaken off her own personal troubles. She woke to life as one man after another walked wearily into the kitchen and dropped, exhausted and silent, into the battered old chairs, and drank her coffee and ate the sandwiches that she had provided. Andrew returned with sliced bread, butter and a variety of cooked meats, all donated free of charge by Mrs Grant, down at the village shop.

'I wonder how it started,' Jeannie said idly. She looked up at the mountain top. The flames would rage there until nothing was left or until rain came and dowsed the fire. There would be thousands of pounds worth of damage. The forestry commission had set several new plantations and there was also wood up there ready for felling. And the beasts . . . it did not do to think about them. Angus had been joined by three of the farmers, and the guns still sounded over the hills. Two stags, several hinds, rabbits, hares, birds, and three sheep caught before the dogs had found them, all lay dead.

There was no sign of the abatement. The men felled the trees and tore away undergrowth, widening the fire-breaks, watching the flames that had spread over all the woods at the top of the Dragon, and had flared towards the first of the Nine Glens, where another gang battled valiantly, and where three farmers from beyond Corrie Beg busied themselves with guns.

It was not possible to dowse a beast that was charred and maddened, and a bird, dying, its feathers burning, might fall in a part of the wood beyond the rides and start off a new outbreak.

Ponies crashed among the branches; squirrels died, as their tails or their dreys caught from a spark; an owl, hooting in panic, flew blindly into one of the men, who beat out the fire from the body and despatched the bird fast. It was too appallingly injured to threaten with beak or claw.

'It's sheer bluidy murder,' Angus said, coming in for coffee.

He was sickened, and fury was mastering him. All the years spent on the hill, all the care guarding the deer, ensuring strong beasts, culling the weaker, coaxing them to breed again on the Dragon, which for too long had been without deer. All wasted.

'If I catch the culprit,' he said, 'I'll break his bluidy neck.'

'Probably campers,' Andrew McKenzie said. 'I heard what sounded like a petrol tank blowing up. I only hope no one is up there, in the woods.'

'I wouldn't care if they were. It would do them good to be here and see those beasts.' Angus could not get them out of his mind. The dying stag, the dead hinds, one of them very late in calf, the others with young at heel and God alone knew where the calves were now. Perhaps lying, as they had been taught, frozen in the bracken, safe hidden from enemies, but roasted by hellish flames. Both hinds that he had shot were full of milk.

'If only it would rain.'

The thought was on everyone's lips, was voiced in the village where the women watched anxiously, lest fire spread towards them. Their eyes looked constantly towards the Dragon.

Men straggled home for brief rest and stumbled out again. Cars roared into the village and their occupants seized axes and made for the mountain. Every hand was needed to fight the monster that bred there under their eyes, that roared its defiance to the unclouded blue, that surged joyously to and fro on the wind, that swept everything before it into its all-devouring maw. The Dragon had come to life and was destroying itself.

'If the fire gets a hold on the lower slope we'll be done for, Jeannie,' Angus said, as she stood beside him. Her small face was white against the dark fringed frame of straight hair, her blue eyes smudged with smoke and soot, and tired. There were no beasts moving now. The place was dead except for the wind-fanned hell that raged against the sky, that had grown so that it was reflected in the steely waters of the loch, far below.

Jeannie could only nod. She had thought that she would never feel anything again, had imagined that for her, life held no future, and that nothing could rouse her to anger, but the dying beasts had shaken her, had torn down the screen of apathy that she had set between herself and the world, and she felt their pain added to hers. She knew that her father's rage

34

would leave him shaken and exhausted. She pitied him and longed to put her hand on his and tell him so, but that was a familiarity that he had never encouraged, too awkward to know how to deal with it.

If the cottage burned ...

She looked up at the Dragon. There was an evil beauty in the blending kaleidoscope colours, in scarlet and orange and gold and yellow and crimson and black, in the smoke pall drifting against the sun, which hung in limbo, dark red and enlarged to twice normal size. There was a hateful excitement in the raging fury, in the surge and sweep and sudden crescendo of the flames, in the leaping light that blazed across the mountain and coloured the day.

'Wind's veering,' Andrew said, some hours later, watching the smoke-spread turn towards the top of the mountain. 'As long as it holds like this the village is safe ... and your cottage too.'

Angus nodded, almost too tired to care. The sun had long been gone from the sky and dusk was challenging the fire. Soon it would be dark, and they would have to stand watch, to see that nothing came out of the trees to set light to a fresh patch of the forest, and to see that the wind did not rise to a gale that would send sparks leaping across the rides, and hurl flaming branches as if they were children's playthings, and sweep the triumphant inferno through house and barn and store until nothing was left of the village of Invernay but a blackened memory that shouted its outrage to the uncaring sky.

When the moon rode high, and looked down at the glare that dulled its soft light, Jeannie crept wearily to bed. She watched the leaping lambent glow, and the flash and flicker that danced on her bedroom walls, and then fell asleep, exhausted by the events of the day, for once not even remembering Robert and all that he had meant to her.

Below Angus cat-napped in an armchair in the kitchen, waiting to be called to take his turn outside, and Andrew McKenzie slept on the battered old couch. His shoulder was painful, and the doctor, who had had to come and stand by permanently to attend to the many burns, had forbidden him to take further part in the fire fighting. He could help Jeannie, and maybe she would remember and in time turn to him and find consolation. Andrew was a patient man, and he could wait, but the hope aroused in him would not be stifled.

Angus slept, his dreams marred by dying beasts that mocked his impotence, and he was thankful when one of the foresters shook him to wakefulness and took his place in the chair and was asleep before he had even had time to put on his boots.

Chapter Five

The hind herd had been feeding at the head of the first of the Nine Glens when the fire broke out. The calves were playful, running in the early dawn, butting and kicking in mock battle, preparing for adult life.

The old hind was anxious. She had smelled the bonfire the night before, and it worried her. There had been fire in the forest when she was young, long ago, a faint and teasing memory. One of her own calves had died in it and she herself had a raking slash of darker fur that hid the scar of a burn made by a blazing branch as she fled beneath it.

She stood on a small knoll, looking towards the smoke. Her eyes told her little, but her sensitive nose warned her not only that there was unknown menace, high on the Dragon, but that man also was there. She caught the stink of bodies and the sharp smell of the beer the lads were drinking, and the stench of frying food. Her ears heard the crackle of wood as it burnt, and the bray of the noisy voices that had already driven the hinds to their secret fastness in the first glen, away from fear and away from danger.

She was ready to alert the herd, to nose the calves from the bracken, aware that this was no time for hiding, but a time for speed. Her hooves were poised to thump a warning, her voice was ready to bark at laggards, her frightened heart thudded against her ribs, as the stench on the wind increased and an eddying breeze brought acrid smoke to sting her eyes.

She stamped. The herd, alerted, were waiting, ears moving, wise brown eyes wide with alarm. This was a danger that none of the other hinds had met before and they did not know how to avoid it.

The grandmother led the way, swiftly rousing hidden calves from the heather, and the other mothers followed her until all the beasts were leaping, panic-mad, down the glen and away from the fire and the terror that stalked them so dreadfully.

Smoke was following them, swirling and eddying, first from behind, chasing some of the hinds, and then from the side, so that those that were caught by it swerved to avoid it, and ran into it, and lost all sense, leaping wildly, thrusting through the dark and stinking mist that had suddenly descended upon them.

Rusty's mother was one of the first to turn away. She made for familiar ground, running desperately towards the bracken clump where her son usually sheltered. She had not seen the old hind nose him from cover, nor had she seen him run, as bewildered as the other beasts, with the main body of the herd, fully able to hold his own and keep up with them.

The grandmother ran sheepdog round her charges, pushing at the little ones, anxious to keep the herd together and take it to safety, away from the clinging smoke and the cloying smell and the wild noises from the burning forest behind her, where the bellows and moans of dying beasts added to the snap and crackle of blazing trees.

There was a freshwater lochan at the end of the first glen. It was shallow, no more than knee deep, and the deer often drank there. She plunged into the water, knowing that here was safety, and the other deer came after her, the calves drawing back from the chill, until the hinds forced them in. They stood wearily, flanks heaving, panting after their run. There was less than half the herd with them. Several calves had run back to their dams, and many of the hinds had dashed away, dizzy with terror, and courted disaster. Some had found destruction, there in the man-made hell that had taken hold of their familiar woods and secret places, there where in October each year the great stags fought for supremacy, where the calves were born and where the herd sheltered.

Rusty, standing beside the herd leader, his own nose telling

38

him of danger, looked for his mother. She had vanished, and he tried to leave the water and seek her, but the old hind chivvied him, knowing his thought. He bleated forlornly, and the grandmother licked his nose comfortingly, but she was barren and could not give him milk and he was not yet weaned, nor would be for several months. He turned to a hind close by and sought to feed from her, but she kicked him angrily and he added the ache of a bruised rib to his fear and his hunger. He stood, head hanging, under the summer sun, and sucked at the water, but it was not what he wanted, nor what he needed. His small body drooped wearily.

His mother, running through the woods, blundered across one of the rides. A forester saw her and yelled, trying to head her back, away from the fire, out of danger, but she mistook his intention and, terrified, plunged into the inferno. She died when Angus saw her leap from the flames, and shot her in mercy.

The fire burned for two days and two nights before rain, drenching from sodden clouds, put an end to it, and all that was left of the trees that crowned the Dragon were blackened stumps, pointing starkly at the sky. The earth smoked and steamed, with never a blade of grass or a leaf of heather. Nothing left for the deer to graze. Nothing left for the grouse to eat, those of them that did not lie, as scorched as the trees, on the dead protesting ground.

Angus, walking in the fields at Corrie Beg, looking over his sheep, glanced at the shore of the loch.

'Aye,' the farmer said, following his gaze. 'I've never seen aught like it. All the beasts have come to the waterside. They only leave the beach to drink from the burns.'

There were sheep, refugees who had not been gathered by the dogs; cows and hinds browsing on seaweed among them, and two solitary stags, who, among the mass of animals, contrived to stand in isolation, their magnificent lordly heads, on which the new antlers thrust, still masked in velvet, looking towards the men.

'They have lost all fear,' the farmer said. 'It's awful weird.

Puir beasties. It must be beyond their understanding.'

There were ponies and hares grazing close to the wall that separated the field from the beach. The hares were wary, noses busy, scenting the wind, ready to run should the men bring guns, but as yet unbothered.

Angus looked at the hinds, gathered together in a small knot at the end of the far field, their eyes watching him. The old grandmother was there. Her wisdom would have saved the other females and the calves, had they obeyed her. Fifteen hinds and eight calves. There had been at least twelve youngsters when he had last seen the little group and there had been over twenty-five hinds. There must have been many calves lost in the fire. There was another herd in the fifth of the Nine Glens. Perhaps the missing beasts had joined them.

He walked towards the deer, curious to see if their caution would overcome their obvious fear of the smouldering hill behind them. It would be days before the ground was cool, or new growth started through the scorched dead vegetation. The villagers were catching up on undone jobs, and life held a semblance of normality for them. Angus would not find it normal for days to come. He had lost the grazing for his sheep and would have to make some arrangement to tide him over the next months.

He had also lost six lambs, dead after the race to reach lower ground, two fallen as the ewes ran, and trampled by the speeding hooves, and the other four exhausted and taken in the night by foxes. And two ewes had also died. If folk only knew the trouble they caused by their blind bloody stupidity, he thought, staring up at the ravaged hill, where the burnt out wreck of the old van shouted human guilt at all who saw it.

One good thing had come from the fire. Jeannie had overcome her misery and was almost her old self again, cleaning the house thoroughly and cooking him a good dinner, a steak and kidney pie, which he loved, with potatoes mashed to fluffy cream and carrots in a sauce that made his mouth water to remember it. She had baked a cake too, and he had surprised her exercising her lame leg, a thing she had not troubled to do before although she had been told it was essential if she was to lose her limp and regain her strength.

She was cleaning up now. Smoke had sullied everything and curtains and blankets and carpets all stank of burnt wood. He could see half the contents of the house blowing on the line that he had stretched for her between the two tall trees that sheltered the garden and that stood, improbably green, beneath the blackened slope.

He turned back to the deer. The calves were frisking together, the hinds guarding them, the old grandmother standing sentinel, her eyes watching him as he strode towards them.

Her hind hoof stamped, imperious summons to flee, away from man, away from danger. The hinds turned, white scuts bobbing as they leaped, and the calves followed them. All except one small beast that lay, nose on tail, eyes lacklustre, scarcely flicking an ear as Angus came towards him.

He was, the man guessed, one of those orphaned by the fire. His coat was rough, and two marks on his ribs showed where he had been kicked as he tried to find a foster mother. The old hind had protected him, but she could not feed him. Now she watched, hesitant, afraid to return, yet unwilling to leave her charge behind.

Angus bent over the little animal. Rusty looked up at him, and his ears moved slightly. The stench of man was overpowering and he turned his head away, and tried, feebly to stand, but his legs did not obey him, and he fell, and looked helplessly up at the giant two-legged creature that stood over him.

Angus lifted the calf as easily as if he were hefting a lamb. He was used to carrying the smaller animals, and he held the deer firmly, arms enclosing the four legs, supporting neck and rump. Rusty was too exhausted to protest, too bemused to care, missing his mother who had always come to him before when he cried for her, who had warmed him and soothed him and fed him, so that he had complete trust. He could not understand why she did not come now, and he bleated pathetically, a small forlorn whimper so faint that only Angus could hear.

41

This would not be the first orphan he had reared. It was not an easy thing to do, nor was it always wise. A wise creature would often not respond to hand feeding and might die. When he was grown he hankered after his own kind, and it was always sad to see him go. Angus had reared three stags and two hinds, and all had returned to the herd, but all had fallen victim to poachers because they had lost their fear of man. It might be better to let the wee beastie die, but that was something he could not do.

'I'll give him to Jeannie to rear,' he said to the farmer at Corrie Beg. 'It will occupy her mind.'

The farmer nodded. He wanted to sort the sheep, and put Angus's flock in a separate field until they found fresh grazing. There was little enough here for his own beasts, so close to the sea, and the ground poor and peaty and thick with soaking yellow-green bog-moss. Just a pittance for each ewe, and now there were deer and ponies and hares all feeding from his land. It was a good job the firemakers had got away, he thought. Lynching was too good for the deils. Damn them to hell for all eternity. His thoughts were bitter as he looked at the Dragon and looked at the beasts crowded on to his own sparse grazing, but his nod to Angus was civil enough. Not his fault after all.

'I'd like to catch yon firemakers and flay them alive,' he said, voicing the thoughts that had been in every mind since the blaze began.

'I wud burn them,' Angus said, and began to climb the rocky path back to the cottage, aching in every bone and muscle, too tired to think coherently, the deer calf, too weak to struggle, a leaden weight in his arms.

'Dad?'

Jeannie's voice questioned him. She had heard him walking heavily, stumbling, but had not gone out, knowing that he would hate his weakness to be observed, just as she hated her own lagleg rousing sympathy. She looked out of the doorway, small pointed face and wide cat eyes serious. Her father was massive in the breeches and thick jacket that he wore when working.

'An orphan?'

Angus nodded.

'Aye. And almost deid.'

'Put him in the shed and I'll find the bottle.' There were always lambs to feed. Jeannie made up a milk mixture and warmed it, and took the wrapped sterilised teat, and filled the bottle that was kept in a metal container ready for immediate use.

She put Angus's food on a plate and went outside and sent him in. He sat, scarcely tasting the food, longing for sleep. When he had finished he poured a tot of whisky and dropped into his big leather chair, while the dogs stretched out at his feet, Star stealing pride of place, his head on Angus's foot. They had always come indoors. His wife had liked them, and she did not spoil them so he let her have her way, although he felt that the animals should be kennelled outside, and not grow used to soft rugs and the luxury of a warm fire.

He slept.

Outside in the shed Jeannie tried to make the deer calf drink, but his fear was greater than his hunger and his trembling body betrayed his feelings. She sat with his head against her, forcing milk into his mouth, but he refused to swallow. She spoke to him, soothing him, but the fright in his eyes would not die, and she did not know what to do. She had never felt so helpless in her life.

Chapter Six

'Leave him alone for a wee while, lass,' Angus said, some time later, looking in at the door. 'He's terrified. He's been taught to fear us, and it will take time to overcome that.'

He looked down at his daughter. She was small and slender, blue-eyed and white-faced, her dark hair emphasising her pallor. She was no longer apathetic, but from the look of the deer calf, she was going to suffer more heartbreak. He had lost the will to live, and unless they could rekindle it, he would die before the week was out. Few young wild animals survived so much shock. There were small burns on his dappled fur, and a scorch mark beneath one eye, but there was little sign of any worse injury.

'He's not going to die.'

All Jeannie's nursing instinct had been aroused, and this small beast had captured her affection. Angus watched her shut the door. She had always been an intense child, feeling hurt far more than most, reacting with savage anger to cruelty or unhappiness, taking flowers to her dog's grave for weeks after he died, and grieving bitterly when the young deer that they had fostered had returned to the wild and suffered death because they trusted man and came forward, curious to see the guns, knowing that Angus had always carried his and never used it on them.

Nothing would ever be easy for Jeannie. She would never take life lightly. Injustice angered her, and when she was annoyed she spoke her mind, just as her father did, and like him, she hated cruelty to animals, and flared into fury at any

44

man who harmed a beast of any kind. She looked back now at the door of the shed.

'Try again in a while,' Angus suggested. 'He will be more used to the place.'

Rusty lay in the straw. It was strange to him, used as he was to the feel of damp earth beneath him and the heather smell, and the scent of bracken and the tang borne on the wind. There was no comforting knowledge of the herd close to him, or safe feeling from his mother, or the old hind, curled against him. No other calf to run with and butt in fun, preparing for his stag days, strengthening his muscles, learning how to live.

It was dark and there were sheep smells and dog smells and the smell of the horses. He sighed deeply, and slept, coming even nearer to death. It might creep over him and absolve him from the need to breathe and grow and feel, and relieve him of the dull misery of loss that absorbed him completely.

He woke, and bleated for his mother, calling so softly that only Fly, the collie bitch, heard him. She paused outside the shed door, one paw lifted. There was a young animal in there, a beast in need of comfort. Fly had mothered orphan lambs and orphan pups and even an orphan hare and her mother instinct was strong. She went to find Jeannie, whining, demanding instant attention.

When Jeannie did not understand, the bitch pawed at her leg, and barked, and went to the door, looking back, begging her to follow. Jeannie went outside, and Fly ran to the shed door and whined.

'She wants to go inside,' Jeannie said. 'She'll scare the baby even more.'

'She might help him. Fly's all mother, and she's good with small beasties,' Angus answered, after watching the bitch scratch urgently at the shed door. 'It can't do any more harm.'

He opened the door and let the bitch inside, watching over the half door after he had closed it. The calf huddled closer to the ground, alarmed by the scent of yet another creature that he had been taught to hate.

45

Fly was not deterred. She went to him, and her warm tongue licked his nose. He opened wide eyes, sensing at once that here was comfort and she meant him well. The tongue was a gesture to all young creatures, a reassurance, and a signal. Fly licked his face and after a few minutes hesitation he put his nose up to hers. She curled in the straw, her body sprawled so that he could lean his head on her and gain consolation from her presence. She was prepared to stay with him as long as he needed her, as she stayed with new lambs until they were ready to fend for themselves.

'Try the bottle now,' Angus suggested. 'He's more at ease. He might even feed.'

Rusty did not like the rubber teat. The smell of it was so strong that it drowned the smell of milk, and as soon as Jeannie came near he began to tremble again. Fly, sensing his unease, whimpered. He pushed his head against her, and tried to burrow into her soft fur. She represented mother-hood, and he needed her, but she could not feed him.

Andrew McKenzie, bringing the mail from the village on his way back to the forestry cottage, saw the group by the shed and came to look.

'Try a rag on your finger, dipped in milk,' he suggested. 'It worked with a wee kitten we found abandoned in the forest. The poor wee beastie was no more than three weeks old. His brother and sisters were dead, but he wanted to survive, and survive he did. Took us all our time to keep him alive at first though.'

Angus went back to the kitchen for an old and ragged towel. He tore it into pieces, and brought it to the shed. Jeannie wrapped it round her finger and poured the milk into a bowl which Angus had brought with him. She put the finger into the deer calf's mouth.

He let it lie for a moment, his wide eyes watching her, and then the warmth and the taste were suddenly familiar and he began to realise that no one meant him harm. He sucked at the soft cloth, and swallowed.

It was a long, laborious and messy process. Twice Jeannie

tried the teat and bottle, but Rusty hated it. The warm milk on the soft cloth wrapped round her finger was all he wanted. The two men left her, and went inside the house, while Fly watched jealously, making sure that her new charge was properly tended.

'It would ha'e been better to shoot the beastie,' Angus said, pouring beer from a can into two glasses. 'He'll no' live.'

'He might.' Andrew went to the kitchen window and looked out at the Dragon. Beyond the loch the mountain ranges massed under the sky, sunlight brightening them, while the wind chased cloud shadows over the slopes. The houses in the village sheltered under the massive shoulder of the hill that protected them from the worst of the weather, and from the wind that tore the Dragon and screamed through the Nine Glens and savaged the trees.

Jeannie was cramped and exhausted long before Rusty had finished the milk. He had not taken much. The cloth absorbed it, and some had been spilt, and most of it wasted, but he had drunk a small amount, and perhaps, with Fly mothering him, he would be more trusting in the morning, and perhaps she could accustom him to the bottle. If only she could mask the smell of the teat, which was, she was certain, deterring him from sucking. Even she could smell the rubber.

She went into the kitchen. Andrew had gone, and her father had cooked bacon and eggs for both of them. She was hungry, and did not realise it until she began to eat. Angus watched her, and sighed thankfully. She had been feeding like a bird for weeks, picking and pecking and leaving good food on her plate and growing thinner and smaller under his eyes. Now perhaps she would make progress too. If only she did not take life so hard ...

He went out to lock up for the night. The deer calf was asleep, his head on Fly's back. He whistled to the bitch to come and feed, but she would not leave her charge and he put her plate in the straw. She was a devoted mother. Always had been, and he knew that she would exhaust herself and starve herself rather than leave a single one of her adopted charges when it needed her. She licked his hand when he put the plate on the floor, and his fingers lingered on her neck. She was one of the most affectionate animals that he had ever known, and worth her weight in any currency in the world. He had had many offers for Fly, but he would as soon sell his daughter. He grinned wryly at the thought.

Chapter Seven

Auld Lexie lived in a hut in the first of the Nine Glens. No one knew who he was or where he had come from, but he had been there for so long that even Angus could not remember a time when the smoke from his fire had not risen above the clearing.

Auld Lexie had built his home from odds and ends. He had furnished it with chairs thrown out from the farm at Corrie Beg, and curtains that Angus's wife had given him, years before, and a table that he had made himself from three planks of wood and two old clothes props.

He was a thin man, a tall man, with a shock of white hair that shone in the sun and stood up round his head like a halo of an improbable saint. His brown face was deeply lined, his eyes mild and deerlike. His overcoat was mended, neatly enough, with multi-coloured wool, and it flapped at his ankles, and was too long in the sleeves, so that everyone wondered what man had worn it before him, as Auld Lexie was nudging six foot, and though thin was broad framed and muscular.

He collected waifs and strays. His small room housed three cats, a blind sheepdog that a farmer beyond Invernay had intended to shoot, as she did not earn her keep, and two more dogs, one a lame whippet with half a foot missing through being caught in a trap, and the other a nondescript mongrel that had been left behind one afternoon by a family in a big car, who had dumped him and driven away and left him howling his love for them, and brought Auld Lexie to cursing impotent fury at the wicked selfishness of folk who bought a dog, because they liked pups, and then, when it was grown and larger and more expensive than they expected, left it to fend for itself. He comforted the beast and added it to his own collection.

He earned money for food for his animals by working on the farms, and helping the foresters. Having no trade, he would turn his hand to anything, and fell trees or chop wood, or keep watch at lambing time. Angus valued him as he had a way with beasts that was second to none, so that they trusted him instantly and he could quiet a terrified ewe in trouble at birth by putting a hand on her head and murmuring to her, while Angus delivered the lamb.

He could quieten ponies and approach closer to the deer than any man that Angus knew, and much of his life was spent leaning against a tree watching the birds and the beasts, seeing the eagle hover high above the Dragon and sweep down for his kill; seeing the hare nurse her leveret, watching fox cubs play at dawn, often coming almost to his feet as he stood, immobile, as much part of the wilderness as they.

Angus turned a blind eye if there were salmon bones in Lexie's midden. The old man did more good than harm. He also helped beat for pheasants, or stalk for deer when the city men came to shoot. He knew which beasts needed culling, and took men to kill the one-eyed or the lame, or those with single antlers, or deformed bodies or heads. Take those from the herd and prevent them from breeding and the new beasts were strong and sturdy and no weaklings were born. Auld Lexie guarded the Master stags jealously. They were needed to father the calves born on the hill, and he told no one where they hid. Often a man from the city could stare a big stag in the eye and not even see him, and Lexie hid his glee, knowing that though these men might think him lacking in brain, he knew much more than they.

They did not know where the vixen hid her cubs, or the wild cat had his lair, or the Hill Master wallowed in the peat hags. None of them could find a basking salmon and lift him from the water so swiftly that the fish was on the bank before he had time to flick his tail. None of them knew where the trout hid in the

50

burns, or knew how to cast a fly so that the fish did not see the man on its skyline. Auld Lexie could fish so cunningly that he remained unseen and the trout rose to the fly as swiftly as if it were a real fly on the water. And the flies that the old man made were miracles of life, aping truth so well that even Angus had been deceived when he saw them.

When Jeannie was small she had loved Auld Lexie, and marvelled at the flies that he made and at the wooden toys he carved for her with his old battered broken bladed knife. She had them on her mantelpiece; a sleek and elegant seal, a cunning donkey, ears pricked forward listening, a squirrel, and a deer hind with a gentle face and kind expression. Auld Lexie could have made a fortune with his carvings if he had desired but he had no use for money and he only carved for those he loved. He also fought for those he loved and had any man harmed Jeannie or one of his animals he would have killed him in rage.

The village was used to him, as he walked down to buy food, or, on the Sabbath, to sit in the graveyard, outside the kirk and listen to the singing. He never went inside, but the minister, knowing he was there, would leave the door ajar on fine days so that he might hear better and the congregation heard the old man's voice echoing the hymns.

He had never married, being terrified of women, and not liking men, who were liable to laugh at him or mock him. Animals were kind, and did not say one thing to a man's face and jeer at him behind his back. He was safe with his beasts and he was safe with Jeannie, who might have been his daughter, and for whom he felt nothing but kindness and affection. She would make some man a good wife, and it would be good to see bairns playing with her. He loved small children, because they trusted him and were too young to laugh at him. When they grew old enough to see him with their elder's eyes he had no time for them. He was a sensitive man and afraid of mockery, valuing himself too lowly.

His world was the hillside and the heather and the high bare peaks where the stags went in summer, and the clearings among the trees planted by the foresters where the hinds

51

bedded down to birth their calves. The windy beach where the waves broke and foam feathered the rocks, and crabs lurked in the orange weed, and seals lifted out of the water and slapped their tails like cannon shot, and the heron stood, statuesque, and watched for little fish, and the hoodies marched, ungainly, turning the weed for carrion thrown up by the receding tide.

He walked on the Dragon and looked at the burnt grass and blackened heather, the stark and ugly outlines of the ravished trees, and the bodies that lay where fire or shot had caught them. Anger choked him, and he shook a furious fist at the burnt out van and sent a rolling Gaelic curse after those who had so outraged the mountain. He read widely, from the old stories of the Brown Seer, a wise man of long ago, whom he reverenced, to the poems of Rabbie Burns and the rolling stanzas of the Border ballads. He could recite *Lord Ullin's Daughter* or *Young Lochinvar* and sadden the men in the bare bar-room as they listened. When he had marred their spirits and silenced them with sorrow, he took his pipes and filled the room with the swirl and lilt of the music, until toes tapped and fingers danced on the wooden tables and voices were raised in singing.

He was in no mood now for music, although he slowed to listen to a bird that poured a lyric from its small throbbing throat, and stopped again to watch a partridge drag a lagging wing, anxious to distract him from its nest, and from the chicks huddled under a dock leaf. He saw bright eyes watching him, but he signalled to the dogs and turned away. They followed, knowing he might favour them and spoil them with titbits, but he would never countenance misbehaviour.

He waited, leaning against a tree, a long grass stalk in his mouth. It tasted of woodsmoke, and he spat it out, while blind Sue leaned against his leg, and the lame whippet, Trip, investigated a mousehole, and Rap, the mongrel, stood close beside him as if afraid that Lexie, too, would desert him. He never let the man out of his sight. It had been too great a shock to be left alone in the wild by people he had trusted.

Auld Lexie was content to be part of the wood. The foresters had given the deer grand cover. He watched, noting a harbouring stag, so still that only the wind teasing the hairs on his ears betrayed his presence. Lexie could see the outline of the growing antlers, hidden in velvet, the two widespread ears, listening to every whisper, every hint, every rumour, picking out the cry of a wheeling gull below, the note of a bird, the sigh of the wind in the grass, the faraway swirl of waves on the stony beach below. He could see the nostrils quiver as they tested the air, which did not betray man or dogs, for the wind was in their favour. He could see the wise brown eyes, the track of tears in the fur, and the flies that clustered, and the scent gland under the eyes. The beast tossed his head, irritated, the whippet, excited, forgot himself and barked, and a moment later the stag was gone, and not even Lexie saw him vanish.

He beckoned to the dogs and spoke to Sue, whose ears answered him. She turned sightless whited eyes and sought the comfort of his hand, and then plodded on, her nose thrusting at each step against his leg, in spite of the lead that held her.

He found Jeannie trying to feed the deer calf, which lay, listless, while Fly caressed him.

'He'll die,' Jeannie said.

'Not he. Ye need a nanny goat, lass. That milk's too rich for a wee deer. I'll bring ye the forestry men's goat. They'll no' be minding. She's full o' milk.'

Angus, overhearing, as he came out of the house after his midday meal, stopped to watch. The deer calf was even nearer to death. Fly could not warm him to life with her affection. He took her comfort but did not respond when she licked his face. He sighed deeply, and every sigh added to Jeannie's despair.

'I'll drive ye over there,' Angus said.

The calf's ears flickered as the Land-Rover drove past, but he settled again. There was a milky film over his brown eyes, his coat was harsh and staring, and his side barely lifted as he breathed. Jeannie could not bear to watch him, and she went indoors and began to tidy the kitchen, but her mind was not on her work, and she broke a cup and a jug and gave up and went to sit on the low garden wall and watch a small boat skim over the loch, its sails catching the wind.

The nanny goat was used to travel. She stood meekly while Lexie held her, and watched the world go by over the tailboard of the Land-Rover. The forestry men also had a cow and they lent the goat willingly.

There was long grass in the orchard, and here she was tethered, and Lexie milked her, crooning to her to keep her still, singing an old Gaelic song that his mother had taught him.

The milk was warm, frothing and creamy. He found a spoon in the kitchen and went out to the shed.

'Open his mouth,' he said. 'Time won't wait for us.'

The warm milk was comforting. The little beast swallowed, and his eyes opened in surprise. He swallowed again, and again. Lexie soothed him with words, and stroked him between each spoonful.

'Poor wee mannie. Poor wee mannie. There now. Drink it doon. Drink it doon. There's a grand wee beastie.'

Jeannie watched. She had forgotten how good Lexie was with animals. He could coax an ailing pony to feed, or gentle a sick cat. He had brought their old Tom back to life after a rat bite had poisoned him, by pouring brandy down his throat after the Vet had said that the cat would die. Tom, incensed by the burning fiery taste, had gulped and swallowed, and half an hour later had licked his paws and washed his face and staggered weakly to a favourite chair and tried to jump on the the seat. A few days later, he was roaming the stacks and keeping the vermin at bay.

'He'll do.'

Lexie put the almost empty bowl on the floor and Fly lapped it greedily, lingering over the corners and the last creamy drops. When she had licked the plate she cleaned her whiskers with a last flick of her tongue, and then washed the calf's face. He leaned against her, and his eyes looked up at Jeannie, accepting her, and the man with her, his fear fading. They had comforted him and fed him and he knew they were trying to help. There was no danger here. The lesson his mother had

54

taught him was becoming dim. He cradled his head on the dog's back and closed his eyes. Fly, utterly content, licked his face again and stretched beside him, guarding him as he slept.

When one of the pointers came nosing at the door, anxious to discover more about the strange-smelling newcomer, she growled softly. Mac had no desire to annoy her and withdrew, pretending that he had urgent business in the orchard corner. Dignity satisfied, he returned to the garden path and stretched across the doorstep, prepared, if necessary, to defend his master's territory with his life.

Lexie looked down at the beasts.

'Try him wi' the bottle to-night,' he said. 'I think he'll tak' it.'

He whistled his own dogs, who had been lying, patient, outside the gate, and walked off down the hill. He wanted no thanks, no sign of gratitude that would embarrass him. Jeannie watched him go, an odd, scarecrow figure, his long coat flapping against his heels, his three rapscallion dogs beside him. His white hair lifted with the breeze. He did not look back.

Later that day she knelt by the deer calf, the bottle of warm goat's milk in her hand, and watched the little beast suck eagerly, tugging and pulling with all the fervour of a young lamb that had been bottle reared. In time Rusty might trust her, might allow her to stroke him and lift him, might play with her and with the dogs, and run in the field with the ponies, as the other young deer had done.

Remembering them, she frowned, and sat glumly over her supper, scarcely seeing the food, until Angus asked her what was wrong.

'We can't let this one go back to the forest,' she said. 'He'll be killed like the others. He'll be too trusting.'

'We can't keep a stag in a paddock,' Angus said. 'When his antlers grow he'll turn wicked. It often happens. He may be safe with us, but he will not like strangers, and we have too many hikers up here in August. And even in the paddock we might not keep him safe.'

'You can't keep anyone safe,' Jeannie said desolately. That

night she remembered Robert, and felt it wrong that she should have forgotten him. Long after Angus was asleep she sat and watched the moon silver the water and shadow the forest, and listened to the wind mourning in the trees. She could keep nothing for ever. The fear haunted her, and she only slept when the first grey light hesitated on the brink of dawn and the birds called the sun from over the horizon, and the mountains flushed briefly in the pale rays that banished the night.

Outside, in the shed, Fly watched the deer calf stretch his legs and stagger to his feet and explore his new home, puzzled by the rough walls and the deep straw and scents that were new to him. His dappled coat was shading into rust. He flicked his ears and dropped beside the bitch and she nuzzled him gently, enjoying her new responsibility.

Chapter Eight

The hot days of June were only a memory. July brought rain, and more rain. Rain that drizzled from a misty sky; rain that swelled the burns and filled the pool beneath the waterfall and lay on the surface of the paddock so that the animals turned the grazing into a muddy .narsh, and Rusty learned to lie on a rock, above the water.

His dappled coat was fading, and the longer hairs of his adult days were hiding the pattern. He ran, the dogs chasing him, until he turned and butted them and chased after them in his turn. Mac, the pointer, in particular, was fond of this game, and the two animals found endless entertainment. Fly watched jealously, but was reconciled when her foster child, now twice as large as she, came to her and nosed her, and leaned against her, needing her affection.

He missed the herd. He learned to trust Angus and Jeannie and to welcome Lexie when he came to see how the calf progressed. He leaned against them, deriving comfort from their presence, and if Jeannie forgot to caress him, he ran after her, bleating, and butted jealously at her until she gave him the petting that he thought his due.

There was another orphan in the paddock with him, a lamb that Angus had found on the high ground, the mother dead from exhaustion. Jeannie reared them together and both waited at the orchard gate when she brought the bottles of milk. Both were impatient. Neither would relinquish the comfort of the warm milk, and the joy of tugging at the teat and draining the bottle dry. If Jeannie forgot them, or was late, or tried to break them of the habit the plaintive bleats soon persuaded her that it was not worth the misery that everyone endured, as small hooves began to kick at the gate and the dogs barked and Fly came, insistent, sure that her charges were being neglected. The nightly ritual was their main comfort, and afterwards they followed quietly and curled together in the shed with Fly guarding them.

Jeannie often left the household duties and watched the small beasts playing. They romped and ran and jumped skittishly, butted in fun, and often thrust together, forehead against forehead, in mock battle.

There was little grazing in the blackened forest. Angus went daily to the field at the edge of the loch, now rented from the farmer at Corrie Beg, and looked over the flock. The damp summer had increased foot troubles, and there was always maggot and fluke to contend against, but in the main the sheep were healthy and did not cause him much worry.

A fox took a lamb, leaving the carcase half eaten. The Vet, passing, thought the small beast had died from pulpy kidney, a frequent ill among newcomers to the flock. Vaccination helped, but did not always prevent it, and maddeningly, the disease attacked the healthiest and most thriving of the lambs. Angus watched anxiously for other deaths, but that seemed to be the only instance and he was glad that he had taken the trouble and expense of vaccinating the ewes in the autumn and again before lambing. In previous years the number of deaths had been high and he could ill afford it.

His wages as keeper were very low, and if he did not farm as well there would be little enough, and Jeannie was not earning. He sighed, and used the neck of his crook to rescue a lamb that seemed determined to throttle itself in a wire, and called the dogs. The dogs could feed on the carcase. He carried it home, cursing at the bad luck that seemed never ending.

The rain became torment. It rained from a leaden sky, day after day, until summer visitors wondered if there was ever a fine day in Scotland. It drizzled and it pelted and it poured, and all the time the wind scoured the Dragon and the blackened slopes were sodden and dismal, and the deer harboured unhappily, wetter than they remembered, in the trees in the Nine Glens, and the stags sought shelter. They had changed their habits, leaving the bare and treeless deer forests for those that men had planted, finding again the joy of deep cover, learning to lose themselves in the shadows so that a man could stand a few feet away and neither hear nor sight them.

Sometimes Rusty saw them, the hinds moving together, seeking better feeding grounds, the calves at foot, the herd huddled against the wet. Feeding was bad, and several times bolder beasts cleared the fence and took hay intended for the ponies, and once Jeannie, looking out into the shadows of a rare moony night, saw a stag, his antlers almost grown, cropping the leaves in the turnip patch. She watched him, and lifted the window, and he turned and gazed at her, head arrogant, and soared over the fence and vanished.

'There will be floods,' Angus said.

He watched the pool lose its outline, watched the water seep and creep over the ground, watched the burns swell in spate and the peaty water foam in torrents so that the mountain was a surge of noise and everywhere a man looked was sodden ground, and as he walked small trickles spurted under his feet. The deer climbed higher, and the sheep were taken to the other side of the loch, halfway up the side of the Blind Man, that was brother to the Dragon, and that did not have so many rills and burns and trickles bursting from its rocky sides. The grazing was poor and the sheep would not fatten, but neither would they drown. There was danger from the burns that fed into the loch, and from the big waterfall behind Angus's house, and from the water that seeped from the ground, making everywhere boggy, and turned some of the marshy places into death traps

Lexie helped to shift the sheep and came to look at the waterfall. It was almost impossible to speak, and the noise of it was a constant reminder and warning of danger. It had never been so full in all the years that Angus had lived at the cottage. It fell over the rocks a scant fifty yards away, and as it widened the earth was eroded and a bigger channel made. Angus looked at it first thing in the morning and last thing at night, and woke in the darkness to hear the sullen roar of racing water, reminding him of an animal that bided its time and waited to engulf its enemies.

He dreamed of water. His clothes were always wet, his feet had not been dry for as long as he could remember and the cottage was filled with steaming clothes as Jeannie tried her best to ensure that he started the day well clad. The rain even seemed to penetrate oilskins. It ensured that the ponies were stabled and bored, as their field became untenable, and Rusty and the lamb quarrelled in the confines of the shed and Fly snapped at them, and the dogs came miserably when they were called, and hurried back to the fireside to lie in the warmth and steam with the clothing.

'I have never known a year like it,' Angus said irritably, when they had reached the middle of August and not known a fine day. It might dawn fine and cloudless but long before midday the rain would sweep over them and blot out the view. The mountain range on the other side of the loch was hidden; the houses were blurred in mist; the trees dripped continuously, and everyone was morose.

Jeannie was afraid of the waterfall. She had never seen it so fierce as it surged and thrust down the rock and drowned every sound near the cottage with its din. Andrew McKenzie, calling in one evening with four fat trout for Jeannie, looked at it in horror.

'That thing's grown to treble its size since I was last here,' he said, his voice raised even though they walked some hundreds of yards from the cottage, where it was no longer possible to speak.

Jeannie nodded miserably. Her nights were haunted by terror. Angus watched carefully, but who knew if a sudden spate or an even worse storm high in the hills might not swell the fall to giant proportions so that it thundered over them in their sleep and carried them all away. Not even the stone of the cottage could stand such a weight of water.

If only the rain would stop . . .

Angus was down in the village the night that the water changed its channel. Jeannie was alone, the dogs lying at her feet. Angus had taken Mac, but left the others behind. They were uneasy. Fly had been whimpering all evening, so that Jeannie had gone out to the shed, aware of the bitch's noise even amid the din of water. Both Tess, the pointer, and Star, the old collie, kept running to the window, and at last Star pawed urgently at Jeannie's leg, and lifted up his head and howled, a noise so eerie and unusual that Jeannie was terrified.

She listened. The sound of the water had changed. Fear possessed her, and she looked out, and saw the first runnel of foam coming over the cliff that was immediately behind the garden. The waterfall was a raging torrent that had broken into three channels, and a fourth threatened her from above.

There was no time to find her coat. She let the dogs out, but they refused to leave her. They nudged at her anxiously, and Star tried to lead her away from the cottage, but the ponies were in the stables, and there were the three animals in the shed. She ran to the stable and released Grey and Bartie, and smacked them on the rump. They needed no further encouragement, and Tess decided to accompany them and drove them up the mountain, angling away from the encroaching water, up to the trees above the fall. They did not need directing. The roar of water terrified them, and sent them panic-wild eyes rolling, whited with fright, up above the danger. When, at last, they were safe, they stood, flanks heaving, head close to head, and Tess sat and watched them.

Fly and Star were with Jeannie. The water was drowning all other sounds, was pouring over the lip of the cliff, was widening. Soon it would overtake the cottage. She did not know what to do. If their home was swept away Angus would come hunting for her and might be killed in the search, but if she went down to the village she might be overtaken by the torrent. She had to go up, and try, somehow, to find a safe way to low ground, and communicate with her father.

The deer calf and the lamb were bewildered, muzzy with

61

the noise in their ears, and alarmed by the fear that Jeannie communicated to them, but the dogs did not hesitate. They had to climb above the danger, had to keep their charges safe, and they herded the lamb and Rusty, heading them away from the foam and smother that was already growing, that was pouring over new channels in the cliff, that was flinging rocks towards them. Jeannie climbed behind the dogs, slithering and slipping, aware that the noise was louder, that the swollen burn had found a new bed, that the trees were alive with creatures climbing higher, climbing above the terror that was drowning the woodlands, hurtling down to the loch, tearing trees from the ground so that they crashed and echoed, and over all the rain fell, driving relentlessly into her face, soaking her, so that she shivered. There was no warmth in this sodden summer, and the ground was soaked and treacherous, and mud stained her clothes.

She crouched on the shoulder of the Dragon, and Rusty, wet and trembling, leaned against her legs and asked for comfort: the lamb bleated forlornly and the collie bitch licked Jeannie's hand, Star moved uneasily, wanting to be even farther away.

Jeannie, looking through the misty dusk, could see the wild white smother of foam. The cliff behind the house was hidden by it, and then, with a roar, cliff and water swept together and the cottage was gone, and only the sound of thunder was left to mark its passing. There was nothing there. Only a surge of foam that flung inexorably downwards, swallowing everything that lay in its track.

Jeannie leaned against a tree and shivered. She was too tired to wonder where they would live, or what Angus would think. She was too tired to wonder if he had been on his way back to her when the cottage vanished, if he had been overtaken by the water, if he had been a victim of the monster that straggled the Dragon and added its ravages to those already caused by the fire. More small beasts were caught in the torrent and died in the flood.

The rain, as if satisfied with the damage it had caused

faded to a drizzle and stopped. The moon peered through a mesh of tattered cloud, shone blandly on foaming water and on scarred hill, shone on the bare rock that the waterfall had scoured before it changed its path, shone on the loch beneath and the lights that pricked out in the village.

A beast moved. There were hinds all round them, under the trees. Jeannie was aware of eyes looking at her, at the dogs and the deer calf. Rusty lifted his head, and saw familiar shapes. He moved towards them, hesitating. Fly lifted a paw.

'Stay!' Jeannie said.

The bitch stopped, puzzled.

The calf moved again, uncertain, his ears listening, as he looked towards the hinds. He remembered them, remembered the comforting smell from their warm bodies, the pleasure of running with his kind. He wanted to be with them, to match his strength against his cousins, to lean against the old grandmother and to lift his face to hers. He remembered his mother and the gentle way she nosed him to cover, and how she greeted him when she returned. He bleated.

A hind answered, the response automatic. Encouraged he moved forward again, the moon lighting the dapples on his coat, not yet completely merged into his adult colouring. Inquisitive heads watched him. He could smell them, and excitement mastered him. He danced a few steps, half trotting, towards them.

Jeannie put her hand down to Fly, who was whimpering, bothered by the strange behaviour of her protégé. The lamb, exhausted by the climb, was curled at her feet with Star guarding him. The clouds were reft from the moon by the wind, which had veered so that the herd caught the scent from the girl and the dogs and the lamb. They looked, curious, uneasy, wary, ears moving, knowing that here was possible danger, was something alien, unusual, needing care.

The old hind, catching the smell of dog, stamped her hoof. The herd fled. Rusty ran after them, eager to be with them, to resume his place among them, anxious to catch them up. He butted one of the lagging hinds. She looked towards him, caught the scent from him, a scent of straw and lamb and dog, of girl, of civilisation. Alarmed, she turned, and her hind hooves caught him full in the ribs, tossing him casually into thorny bramble, where he lay, bewildered, and called his forlorn misery to the half moon that watched the Dragon and dappled the trees and mottled the water with light.

'Good girl,' Jeannie said, and Fly ran to him and licked him and he bleated to her, telling her his desolation. When Jeannie went to him and lifted him, he limped slowly, his bruises paining him, and looked after the running herd, his hurt showing in his eyes. Jeannie fondled him, but he did not want her. He sighed deeply, and limped back to the lamb and curled beside him. Both small beasts were tired. They had climbed high, slipping and sliding over wet ground and slimed rocks, and it was late. It was too dark to find a way to the village. Better not risk a broken leg.

Jeannie crouched uncomfortably beside the animals, thankful that at least the rain had ceased. It was far from warm, and she was glad when Star came and leaned against her and licked her face. Rusty did not acknowledge her. He had been cast out by his own kind, and he wanted to go back to them. Men were a poor substitute for the windy hills and the running games and the company of beasts of his own sort.

She looked down on the torrent that roared where her home had been, and looked down on the village. She was worried about her father. She jumped at the sound of galloping hooves, and Rusty lifted his head, wondering if the herd had returned to him, but it was Tess, who had scented her mistress and brought both ponies. They had been tied in the stables, and both wore halters. Jeannie petted them and tethered them, each to a tree, and settled to watch the night go by and the day dawn on a hillside so desolate that she looked down in sheer terror, unable to decide how she could bypass the torrent and reach low ground. The burns had met in the night, and they covered the Dragon and thrust and foamed and frothed to the sea far beneath.

She looked upwards and saw ten stags etched against the

sky, high above the treeline. Their antlers were almost grown, and the velvet hung from them, tattered and torn, in long ragged ribbons, where they had thrust and worried at trees and at heather, trying to scour the bone clean, and rid themselves of irritation. Rusty lifted his head and looked up at them, at the great beasts that stood, statue-still, and then moved slowly, unafraid, one stag following another, until each vanished, hidden by the rocks that pierced the cloud that veiled the peaks. Rusty lowered his head. They had gone and he was alone again, living among aliens. His eyes were bereft.

Angus's words were clear in Jeannie's mind.

'It is not always wise to take a beastie from the wild.'

She shrugged.

It was too late now. He was hers, and she had to guard him as his own kind had rejected him. She had no choice.

She sighed, and looked down the mountain again, and shivered. Perhaps the dogs would find a way to the loch-side. Or perhaps it might be better to climb to the peak, and find a track down into Nine Glens, where Lexie might help her to get back to the village. Perhaps Lexie was dead and the whole of the Nine Glens was awash. It had rained enough.

She spoke to the dogs and untied the horses, and holding their halters, she began to search for firm ground and a way to the road. The dogs nosed the deer calf and the lamb from the ground. Rusty looked back, but there was no sign of deer on the hill. He followed, limping from the kick that the hind had given him, and, wearily, the odd little group stumbled over rock and slipped on mud and blundered through wet heather, unable to find a path that would lead them to safety. The deer and the lamb and the ponies had grazed in the dawn, but the girl and the dogs were hungry. They stopped once, to drink, and then plodded on, and the whole of the Dragon was alive with the terrifying sound of moving water.

Chapter Nine

Auld Lexie was watching the sow at corrie beg. He was in-
valuable at farrowing time. The farmer could trust him to
help in emergency, to breathe life into an apparently stillborn
piglet, to soothe the old sow and watch she did not overlie her
young. Lexie had worked with pigs in his young days, long ago,
longer than any man now alive in the village could remember.
He knew them, understood them, and he loved them.

He watched old Minnie as she lay, flanks heaving. Five
piglets had been born, sturdy, lively, curious, looking up at
him at once with wide eyes, more fully developed than most
mammalian young. Each leaped, in turn, to his feet, and trotted
round the sow and stared up at her, at her mammoth face,
looming above them, at her eyes, friendly but distracted, as
she heaved yet another piglet into the world, at her twitching
ears, at her vast flanks.

The sight never failed to amuse Lexie. He wondered what
the little pigs made of their mother, what they thought of her,
at that first astonishing glimpse. All little pigs behaved the
same way, probably an unerring instinct designed to get them
swiftly out of the sow's way. He was always amused when
they found their milk, and lay tugging, vigorously alive, in-
credibly active, amazingly intelligent.

There was no end to the ingenuity of a pig. They could learn
to outwit an electric fence, could steal food from an electrified
trough designed to moderate their feeding, sucking swill between the pulses, cunningly taking in twice as much as a breeder
thought they needed to fatten at a reasonable rate.

The seventh piglet dropped to the ground. Lexie waited for movement, but he showed no sign of life. He picked up the warm body, murmuring to the sow, who was alert enough to watch him suspiciously. There was nothing obviously wrong. He inserted his finger into the small mouth, and then breathed deeply into the little beast's lungs. Within less than a minute an answering movement of the ribs reassured him, and the tiny creature gazed up at him and yawned, its red mouth gaping.

He grinned and put it down and it walked unsteadily to the sow's head. He rubbed the damp back with his finger, and it looked up at him, considering this second creature looming into its new and highly peculiar world. One of its brothers was investigating the wooden side of the pen, a baffled look on its face. The sow grunted and the ninth piglet followed the eighth. She usually managed between thirteen and sixteen. She was a good sow, old Minnie.

Lexie had presided at her birth too, and at her mother's.

If only the farmer at Corrie Beg would give him a pig of his own to keep. But it needed feeding and he had not enough money to ensure more than starvation diet. The dogs would fare ill enough if Angus did not help out with rabbits and with meat that his own dogs could spare. Lexie drifted into a dream, a dream in which he owned a pig farm of his own, of fine fat beauties, housed in perfect surroundings, in the most palatial modern sties, with farrowing crates and creeps that kept the sows from hurting the young, with a balanced diet and a man to muck out, while he stooped over the pens and scratched the fat backs and watched his beauties fatten . . . Danish Landrace, perhaps; or Middle Whites, or Large Whites. He did not care for either Berkshires or Tamworths with their forward pointing ears and odd expressions, and perhaps not the Middle Whites either, with their flattish faces and smug looks. No, it would be the Landrace, or the Large White . . .

Minnie grunted again and he returned to reality and spoke to her. She watched him and he counted the little pigs. Ten now. Not many more minutes. Minnie was always quick. He had already been with her for several hours. The first two had arrived before he had. It was milking time, and the farmer had had to go. The cows were only now walking back to the pasture. He heard them lowing.

It had been raining for weeks. He could remember nothing like it, not in all his years. Eighty was he, or was it eighty-two? He could no longer remember and it did not matter. No one would put him down at more than a spry sixty-five. That came of living frugally, and drinking nothing but whisky and not much of that. It cost too many pence these days. Once he'd been able to afford a tot with the best . . . he remembered betting the piper from Inverary that he could down sixteen double whiskies and walk in a straight line on the wall beside the loch, and he'd done it too. He'd had a braw head in those days. He rescued a tiny piglet that was being bitten by an over enthusiastic brother, and put her at the end of the line. The rain drummed on the roof above his head, and fell in sheets past the door, and there was a roar of water such as he had never heard . . . and, dear God, it was coming from the Dragon.

He left the pig and ran to look, ran back to the pig, and then, almost demented, yelled to the farmer, who came running, his face white.

'The hill's collapsed and taken Angus's cottage with it,' he said.

'And Angus and the lass . . .' Lexie could barely speak.

'Angus was buying stores,' the farmer said. 'He went past ten minutes ago, and waved. He will be at the shop . . . the lassie was in the house.'

Lexie stared at the wall of water that massed on the mountain, frothing white, churning over the cliff, making a new road for itself, hurtling towards the loch, bringing down trees that obstructed its path, flinging rocks as if they were bubbles, hurling the shed behind Angus's cottage over and over in a twisting mass of rubble that disintegrated as the water vented its wrath.

'There's not a thing ye can do,' the farmer said. His thoughts ran away with him. Lexie had been fond of the lass, like a grandfather to her. A strange man, Lexie. Some said he had loved a girl in his youth and she had left him on the wedding eve and run off with a neighbour's son and he'd had nothing to do with women since. Would not trust one of them, but Angus's lass had found her own way into his affections, and not surprising, a bonnie wee girl she'd been, and a bonnie big one, too and a shame about her young man. Some folk were born unlucky and maybe Jeannie had been meant to die in the car crash, and having stayed alive, this had happened. If there was a day with a man's name on it, then he had to go, and you could not cheat death. Tom McDuff was a man who believed in Fate, and was not certain that there was any kind of deity other than a malign one that ensured a man might have one or two good times in his life, and the rest all bad ones. It was never easy, farming . . . always some beast ailing, or dying on a man when he least expected it, and not much good fortune. And Angus had less than most . . . he would be out of his mind.

Angus had been standing in the store discussing the rain when he heard the swelling roar. He ran to the door with the garage owner and the postmistress on his heels and watched for a tortured minute before the significance dawned on him.

'Jeannie!' His face was grey, his eyes losing all life, so that he aged in front of the watchers. 'I must go back.'

'For God's sake, Angus, man, there's not a thing ye can do. Maybe the lass heard it and got out and is making her way up the mountain . . . we'll go and look, but ye cannot go near the house. There is nothing left. If the water came down on top of her she had not a chance . . .'

Angus could not stand idle. He had to go and look, had to find men to accompany him to the mountain, had to search the hillside towards the Nine Glens. If she had gone the other way she would have had no chance. She had to be safe. He could not bear any other thought.

The men came. With them were the minister and the farmer

and the schoolmaster, and Lexie would have come too. He watched forlornly, but he could not keep up, his legs were so old, and he had to stay with the sow. For the first time in his life pigs did not seem important. If the lassie were dead . . .

The women stood in the village street staring at the mountain, ravaged and blackened by fire, gouged where the earth had slopped, torn by the white surge of water that thundered down. They had no words to say. They had all known Jeannie. She had played with their daughters, had laughed and talked with them when she came to the store, in the old days before she went away to nurse. Now she was buried in the wreckage of her home. There was nothing to say. Sighing they went indoors, but the roaring water drew them, and more often than not they stood at the window, shuddering as the torrent spilled towards them, afraid even though they knew that the loch would take all that water and more, and that they themselves were safe. Even the children were quiet, looking up at the fall that had not been there the day before, and the gash in the mountain.

'If the trees had not burned the mountain would not have slipped,' Lexie said, but he said it to the sow and she only grunted, as her young tugged at her, and she lay in the rapture of new motherhood and uncaring ignorance.

The cars raced from the village, the men driving round the edge of the sea, cursing the time that it took to reach the far side, eyes on the wall of water that poured in a relentless mass into the southern end of the loch, eyes on the Dragon itself lest new landslips occurred.

Angus drove his Land-Rover as if he were a demon loosed from hell. Mac crouched in the back, swaying and swinging, bracing himself against the curve and slide as he slithered on the floor, or was flung down when they cornered, or when Angus braked. Dark was dropping over them, drifting into the sky, hiding the black and riven slopes, while the thrusting savage water glowed with wild life of its own, glittered in the light of a moon that had not been seen for days, thundered downwards, tearing tree and bush and shrub from the ground, and the men saw the brutality and shivered.

Angus had forgotten caution. He did not know where to look. Did not know whether Jeannie lay in the ruins of the cottage, or was being battered beyond recognition in the wicked turmoil of the water, or lay bruised and broken on the side of the Dragon. He did not know if the hill had slipped without warning, or had sent a grumbling call of danger that she might have heard.

He sped on. Behind him, in the mirror, he saw the lights of other cars. Of the police car, summoned by the constable, from the town, of the Land-Rover belonging to the three foresters who had been in the store with him. He wondered if Andrew McKenzie knew what had happened. There were more lights behind him now as men took their bicycles and motorcycles, and asked for lifts from their friends or employers. There would be men hunting on the Dragon all night. If she was alive they would find her. She had to be alive . . .

The road ended in a mass of earth that blocked it for farther than a man could see. His headlights showed the gash and gouge and slide in the hill. He braked sharply and hooted. Behind him the other men stopped too.

They met beside the Land-Rover. Angus could not speak and he could not swallow. Suppose the lass were under that . . . dear Heaven, half the hill had gone.

One of the policemen came up to him.

'If she got out she would have had to climb,' he said. 'We can search towards the Nine Glens. That's where she'll make for. We'll probably find her before daybreak.'

Angus nodded, he did not believe the man. He could not look away from the mound that rose for over eighteen feet, as near as a man could guess, into the sky. They would all be dead. The lass and the wee deer calf and the dogs, faithful Fly, and brave little Tess, and Star. And the ponies. He had nothing left. No home, no place to go, no child, no beast, except for the sheep high on the Blind Man and they were small comfort.

'Come away, Angus.' The minister was a wise man who knew that sanity lay in occupation. He flashed his torch on to the path up the Dragon between the pines. It was steep and dangerous and slippery.

No one knew where to look. They came to the edge of the gash and stared in horror at the tumbling water that filled the gap where the house had stood. There was nothing left, not even a memory. The house, the garden, the paddock, the orchard, the stone wall and the outhouses, all had slipped away and become a mass of tossing wreckage. Not a picture remained, nor a stick of furniture, not a single treasure to remind him of the past. If only he had stayed . . . if only he had thought . . . if only Jeannie had come with him. It was easy to be wise by hindsight. Mac pushed a cold nose into his hand. He had forgotten the dog and the beast knew it and was jealous of his preoccupation. He fondled the soft ears, and the pointer plodded on, satisfied.

The wind that always swept along the flanks of the Dragon teased at his clothes and hair. Memory teased with it. Jeannie had hated wind. He remembered her as a tiny girl creeping out of her own bed into his and into the safety of his arms, listening with wide eyes, her small body shaking.

'It can't hurt ye, lass,' he had said, over and over again, until at last she slept, cradled against him, and the remembered warmth and trust of the child was worse than a knife twisted in his brain.

He turned away. The moon had thrown off the rags of clouds and poured light on the Dragon, dapple and shadow making the hidden places among the trees traps for the unwary, who thought they saw the girl curled asleep and ran forward, only to find that the gleam had betrayed their eyes and the shine was from flowers or from water that had seeped into pools among the tangled tree roots.

They had reached one of the roads that the foresters used. A vehicle was rocketing towards them, headlights blazing, gears crashing. It bucked to a stand and Andrew McKenzie jumped out, his face drawn with fear.

'Angus. You weren't there. Thank God. Is Jeannie all right? No one seems to know.'

72

They looked at him.

'Was she in the house?' He wanted to shake Angus, to wake him out of the trance that appeared to have seized him, until he realised that they knew no more than he, that their presence here meant they were searching, that she might be safe, or she might be dead, or she might be hurt. He wanted to yell at the moon, to take the Dragon and wring it with his hands, to break and bruise and hurt. He shook his head to clear the jostling thoughts and forced himself to think logically. If she had got away, she would have had to climb. There was no other way past the obstruction. She might have made for the shoulder above the First Glen. Or for Lexie's hut.

He could see her so clearly, her small slim figure, her white face, with the wide eyes, the enchanting cat eyes, fringed by long dark lashes. He had never touched her, never kissed her, never told her his secret thoughts, his hopes. He wanted her to forget Robert. But if she felt for Robert as he felt for her, she would not forget and there was no hope for Andrew McKenzie. He left the Land-Rover and began to plod up the hill and the wind in the trees cried 'Jeannie' over and over.

Mac was following Angus, close at heel. He stiffened, cocked his head, ears forward, listening. The wind was veering, and he had heard a murmur, a whimper, a voice that he knew. He barked, making the men jump. Angus, thinking the pointer had seen a deer, spoke sharply, but Mac forgot him and bounded forward, and barked again, urgently, savagely, with all his might, sending his voice up into the darkness, sending a message that he knew must be heard, sending strength to Jeannie, who heard it, faraway, and recognised the dog's voice.

Tess jumped up. She barked in answer, but only Mac heard. The men's ears were too insensitive to pick up the noise above the sound of water and the moan of wind and the creak and groan and rustle of the trees. Mac ran forward.

'Find him,' Jeannie said to Tess. The sound brought hope. If Mac was there perhaps her father was safe. That the dog was alone and looking for her was a thought that she would not tolerate and she pushed it away before it had time to take shape. Tess ran down the hill, branches tugging at her, thrusting into her face, as she sped towards the other pointer.

The two met some hundred yards from the men. Tess whined and whimpered and rubbed against the dog, and he, overjoyed at finding her safe, and anxious to make Angus understand that here at least was one of the family, barked himself hoarse so that the men came running, stumbling up the hill, falling over tufted heather, tree branches springing back into their faces, sodden bracken soaking their clothes, raindrops spilling off the trees into their hair and faces.

The moon shone on the two pointers. Tess was beside herself, running a short way towards Jeannie, who was far above her and out of sight, and then returning to Mac, licking his face, nudging his nose, rubbing against him. Angus saw her and called, and she flew to him, leaping against him, licking his face too, her tail wagging the whole of her body, unable to contain her pleasure or to keep any part of her still. She moaned with ecstacy, delighted to see him again.

'Where's Jeannie?' Angus said, when the bitch had quieted and he had rewarded her with a fuss, knowing he would get no sense from her until he had shown that he appreciated her rapture.

Tess looked up at him, and ran a little way up the slope. She looked back, and the men in the clearing knew hope for the first time. The girl must be there, surely. The pointer was asking them to follow.

Tiredness was forgotten. They climbed the hill to the shoulder of the Dragon, and Tess ran ahead and came back, and nosed Mac, and butted at Angus and then she barked, and Fly hearing her, answered.

Angus shouted through cupped hands.

'Fly. Fly, lass. Star. Star, lad.'

Both beasts barked, and the lamb hearing a familiar voice, woke up and bleated, always anxious to do as the dogs did, and apparently not at all sure of his own identity. He had never seen another sheep. He ran to the edge of the little ledge of

74

grass that they crouched upon and looked down and his small woolly face was the first thing the men saw.

'If the dogs are safe . . . ' but Angus dared not voice the rest of the thought. They might have escaped, might have broken free, might have got away without Jeannie. Perhaps she had stopped to release the animals and had been caught in the torrent herself. And there was no sound from Rusty who often bleated when the dogs barked. Perhaps both were missing. He dared not hope.

Andrew McKenzie was climbing above them. He looked up and saw the lamb and Tess raced past him, and he heard Jeannie's voice murmur. She was too tired to move, to call out, or to stand. If Mac were there her father was safe and that was all that mattered. It did not occur to her that he must think her lost. She put her arms round Rusty, who was leaning against her, and shivered. It was so cold, and she had been too long lying on the damp ground. Her legs were cramped and the lagleg would not work. She had had to rest. She was exhausted.

'Jeannie.'

Angus was calling to her, and she called back but her voice was a whisper, a murmur, a tremor on the air, drowned by the noises of the night and the sudden urgent hunting call of a belated pair of owls who had lost touch with one another and were recording the fact for all to hear, uttering long mournful hoots.

She must move. She tried to stand, but it was useless.

Her blood seemed to have frozen in the night and chill made her shake. She had never felt so cold in her life. She had not even taken a coat.

Angus pulled himself up the last few feet and clambered on to the ledge. There were tumbled grey rocks all round them, and he could look down the dizzy slope to the far away mirror of the loch, bright with moonlight, and up over the shoulder and down to the shadowed recesses of the first of the Nine Glens. He pushed aside the dogs and knelt beside his daughter. For once he did not even stop to think but took her and held her as if he would never let her go and she leaned against him, thankful to be safe, feeling once more the perfect trust of a small girl guarded against all danger, secure in her father's arms.

Andrew McKenzie, watching them, was jealous. He had no right to go to her, or to acknowledge the delight that swept over him when he saw that she was safe.

'The poor bairn's frozen,' one of the policemen said, and came forward and wrapped his thick coat around her.

'I've brandy,' a voice said from the darkness, but the policeman shook his head.

'She'll be suffering from exposure, and ye never give alcohol for that. We must keep her warm and get her safely into bed, and fast. We'll have to lift her down the hill.'

'She only weighs as much as a calf,' Andrew said. 'Let me carry her.'

He took her, wanting to hold her for ever and protect her for ever and to keep her with him. He dared not speak. She lay limp as a rag doll, and shivers racked her so that he was terrified for her, but afraid to hurry lest he slipped and harmed her. He was aware of the animals following, of the deer calf and the lamb, with Tess and Fly herding them, of the ponies which the minister had untethered, and was holding by the halters, one on either side, butting and slipping, of the men who had now discovered that Jeannie was alive and who were talking among themselves, light-headed with relief.

The Land-Rover was a more than welcome sight. The men piled their coats on the floor and put the girl down gently and covered her. Fly whimpered, Rusty was bleating and miserable, and Angus lifted the deer and the lamb and the dogs jumped in after him, and Andrew backed and turned and drove towards the loch, wishing that he had wings and could fly, that the rough road was a better track, that he dared go fast. Exposure could be fatal and she'd been out there all night on the windy hill, lying in the wet, and not so long since her road accident, and not so long either since she'd worked as hard as any of them through the misery of the fire on the Dragon. It was truly an unlucky year.

The warmth of the coats covering her was soothing, and so was relief from worry, and Jeannie fell asleep, with Rusty lying beside her, his nose on her hand, as much in need of comfort as she. His own kind had rejected him and he had not forgotten.

Dawn was gliding over the mountains when Andrew drove into the village. Light swept over the tops and gilded the hillside and showed the torrent that straddled the Dragon and scythed through the gap where the cottage had stood. He shuddered.

'Bring her to the manse,' the minister said. 'There's room for all of you. The beasties can sleep in the barn. There's straw there that we can spread for them. And we have beds to spare.'

The manse was beside the kirk. Angus climbed out of the Land-Rover and lifted his daughter, and began to walk up the path to the house, the minister's wife opening the door long before he reached it.

As he climbed the steps the kirk door opened. Lexie came out, his head bowed. He had helped with the pigs, and left them safe, the farmer's wife in charge, and spent the night on his knees, feeling that this once the Lord would not mind if he went inside the holy place, even in his ragged old working clothes. He lifted his head and saw Angus and he did not know if the girl were alive or dead. The minister saw his stricken face.

'She is all right, Lexie,' he said.

Jeannie opened her eyes and smiled at him.

'The Lord be praised,' Lexie said, and went back to the farm to muck out the pigs, having completed his self-imposed vigil, sure that the Lord had heard him and taken note of his prayers. The following Sabbath his voice was lifted even louder as he sat on the tombstone under the window and followed the hymns, one bar behind and out of tune, but filled with fervour.

77

Chapter Ten

The search on the hill had been reported over the police car radio. Not only police were listening. A young reporter, on holiday from Glasgow, was playing idly with his landlady's wireless set, when he picked up the message. Within minutes of hearing it, he had joined the search party and learned the story from one of the villagers.

He was there when Angus found his daughter. City bred, he stared incredulously at the odd assortment of refugees. The wet and weary ponies, heads down, herded by the pointer bitch; the black-faced lamb with his speckled coat and his three black legs and his bright inquisitive face, nuzzling up against the dog and the tiny deer, unafraid of either. The two collies, and the girl. He was fascinated by her, and attracted by her white face and smudged eyes, and determined he would see more of her. He did not notice Andrew McKenzie until the man lifted Jeannie and walked off down the track, careful not to slip or stumble, and the small procession of animals followed.

It was too good a story to miss. He might, if he were lucky, make the midday edition of the evening papers. He borrowed a motorbike, and rode off to the village call-box, and managed to reach his editor. The story of the girl who escaped in the eleventh hour and the fifty-ninth minute from utter disaster, taking with her a Pied Piper collection of animals, roused countryside interest, and before Jeannie had time to recover there were reporters calling. The doctor would not let them see her, but the minister's wife allowed them to photograph the lamb and the deer feeding from their bottles, and gave them a picture of Jeannie, taken the year before she went away to work in the London hospital.

Angus had been to see the Laird and had been given another cottage, this time on the outskirts of the village. From his new home he could see the loch, and look up at the torrent that now gashed the Dragon. It would be a long drive to the mountain for each day's work. Round the head of the loch and along the road and up the forestry track to the Laird's lands. But they would be safe. He had no desire at the moment to live again on the mountain. The place had once belonged to the factor but it had been empty for years and was almost derelict. There was no lack of help to put it in order. The men came in the evening when their day's work was done, and tiled the roof and pointed the stonework. The village joiner replaced the rotting wood of the window frames, while Angus himself repaired the floor and glazed the windows. Lexie scrubbed and cleaned, until all that was left to do was whitewash the walls and to think about furniture.

Jeannie recovered after a few day's rest. There was plenty to do in the big old manse, and she helped the minister's wife and looked after the beasts, and was surprised there one morning by Nelson Gunn, a young American, who had read the story of her escape in the newspapers and who wanted to see for himself. He had finished college the previous year and come to England for experience overseas before joining his father as a business consultant in New York.

He watched Jeannie feeding the deer calf, and patted Fly, who had come to inspect him and decided he was trustworthy. Nelson was staying at a guest house in the village beyond the Nine Glens and was bewitched by the high hills and the dark green heather, now splashed with purple flowers, by the burns that criss-crossed the peat and tore in spate to the sea lochs, and by the bays of white sand where the waves splashed against black cliffs and all the troubled history of Scotland was represented by the ruined castles that guarded the sea.

He went away, but he did not forget her. He bought stamps in the post office and heard how she and Angus had lost their home, and had nothing left, not a stick of furniture or piece of cloth, not a picture, not a plate.

The next day a crate arrived at the manse, addressed to Angus. He opened it bewildered, and found inside a dinner service and a tea set, coffee cups and saucers, a tea pot and a coffee pot, egg cups and a frying pan, and three saucepans of different sizes.

'Who can have sent it?' he asked, his face worried. 'I would never buy china like this . . . and I cannot pay for it.'

'There is a card inside,' said the minister peering at it short-sightedly and Jeannie handed him his spectacles.

'It just says, "Good luck. I hope this will help you." It isn't even signed,' he said. 'Someone has read about your bad luck, Angus, and sent you this. It's probably some firm that wants a bit of free advertising.' Modern life made even a cleric cynical at times.

Jeannie looked at the cups and the plates, but they all bore different trademarks. She never knew, as long as she lived, that she owed the gift to an American who had fallen briefly in love with her hair and eyes and the expression on her face as she fed the deer, and the small beast leaned against her, in absolute trust.

The story of the gift went round the village, and many people found that they had a chair or a sheet or a pillow to spare, and the Laird sent carpeting that covered both down-stairs rooms and the hall and stairs, and Angus stained the bedroom floors and the minister found three rugs that had been given him by an old lady who had died, that he had never needed to use.

'I wish I had not lost the beasts that Lexie carved for me,' Jeannie said, and discovered that Lexie had been busy again and still had his old skill and there was a seal for the mantel-shelf in her room and a deer calf waiting for her on a table in the front room that overlooked the loch.

The Laird, who was very old, but kindly, sent pictures from the castle walls. A gloomy glen, in which a stag thrashed his antlers in the heather, and a still life of a grouse and a duck and vase of flowers, a woman's glove, and a gun. Jeannie counteracted them with a bright calendar that the post-mistress found, left over from last year's Christmas stock, and Andrew bought her a picture for her own room, a picture of the fourth of the Nine Glens, painted by a man from Edinburgh. She did not know that he paid more than a week's wages for it, but it greeted her when she woke, and was the last thing she saw at night, and reminded her of the view from the cottage on the Dragon.

They moved in the last week of September. Both Angus and Jeannie felt shut in, there in the valley, always within sound of the sea, that was angry with coming winter and gales that blew spray on to the windows, and sometimes flung water over the road, so that seaweed made the surface treacherous. The mountains were above and behind them, closing the sky, and the noise of the trees on the slope was different. The wind wailed miserably, moaning in the branches, and did not blow so roughly or with such joyous boisterous vigour as on the Dragon.

There was a small paddock beside the cottage and here Rusty and the lamb, now named Speck, played endless games. Rusty seemed to have forgotten his kind. Perhaps he thought he was a lamb, or perhaps a dog. Jeannie did not know. Both the deer calf and the lamb followed at heel. Both would wait when the dogs waited, and both warned her of intruders, bleating loudly whenever the dogs barked.

Angus was often away. He had to keep watch on the Dragon, to guard the grouse and the deer, to make sure that no poachers came from the town and shot over his territory. He had a long way to go now and he was tired and morose. Gunmen from the cities were abroad on the hill. Deer vanished and so did some of the sheep.

Andrew McKenzie called whenever he was free, but Jeannie had no mind for him. She was glad of his company, but he had always been part of her life, and she thought little of his visits. Nor of the visits of Davie Grey, the Glasgow reporter, who came up on his motorbike whenever he had enough time to

81

spare. She had obtained another copy of Robert's photograph. It stood beside the wooden seal on the mantelpiece and his memory was vivid, though less painful.

The young American wrote home about the girl who had escaped with her life and her menagerie and the story so intrigued his parents that they determined to visit him and to spend part of the time touring Scotland and see their ancestral home for themselves.

They arrived at the village hotel early in October, when the Dragon was alive with the anger of the stags and the Hill Master challenged all comers and wallowed in the peat hag, flinging black mud over his back, cooling his fever. He loomed above all lesser stags, his antlers many branched and massive. No other beast answered him when he lifted his head and the bony points lay along his back, and his maned shoulders swelled, and he roared defiance, calling to all quarters of the hill, daring any other male to oust him from supremacy, to seize one of his harem. He ran sheepdog round the hinds endlessly, not wishing to lose any of them, and the little herd grew, as he raged above them, policing his territory, always vigilant.

James and Ellen Gunn had never been in so wild a place before. They stared up at the Dragon, at the blackened slopes and scarred and damaged trees, at the torrent that poured through the gap in the rock and tossed in a white smother of foam down the mountain to end in a pool where the water boiled and hissed and then creamed downwards over craggy ledges until it reached the sea.

They listened to the stags roaring, and the clash of bone on bone as antagonists fought at night. They smelled the tang of brine and seaweed, and shivered in the bleak rooms of the stonebuilt hotel, where logs blazed in huge old-fashioned fireplaces but did not warm the air, and Ellen, used to central heating, huddled close, her feet in the hearth.

Lexie, anxious to entertain the visitors, and show them due hospitality, met them one morning as they walked by the low sea wall, watching two seals who surveyed them inquisitively, standing on their tails in the water.

82

'They look like two old men in a bath,' Ellen said, and laughed as Lexie approached them, and swept off his ancient cap.

'Good morning to you, mistress. Good morning to you, sirr,' he said, emphasising his brogue for their benefit, and Ellen Gunn was instantly enchanted by the burr of his voice, and his beautiful manners. Men of his sort were much brasher in the country. She had never met a man like Lexie before.

'Ye'll be the American lady and gentleman from the hotel,' Lexie said, knowing perfectly well, but anxious to find some kind of introduction.

James Gunn nodded. He was as tall as Lexie, but much broader built, his head massive, its thick bristling mane of white hair tossing in the wind, dark brilliant eyes looking from under brows that flared upwards. Restless, inquisitive, and dominantly alive, James Gunn had a personality that intimidated most men. Ellen, small, dainty, her white hair perfectly dressed, her clothes elegant, had only to raise an eyebrow, and her husband turned to her meekly, although no one else found him in the least accommodating.

'Gunn. That is a good Scots name,' Lexie said appreciatively.

'My great grandfather came from somewhere in the North West of Scotland,' James Gunn said. 'We don't know the exact place. And my wife's grandmother was named MacGregor.'

'Morag MacGregor,' Ellen said. She had adored her grandmother and the tales she told of her girlhood in this country of mountain mists and roaring stags, of men who shot over the moors at grouse, of picnics that the women and children shared when the shooting parties stopped for lunch. Of life in the home of her cousins, an ancient and chilly castle where the wind soughed in the trees, and the old stones let the draughts through and it was terrifying to hold a candle and watch the flame blow flicker-fast in the huge rooms at bedtime, where the children crept into canopied beds and closed the curtains, always afraid that an ancestral ghost might creep in and peer at them as they waited for sleep.

83

'Morag MacGregor,' Auld Lexie said. He put one foot on the low sea wall and looked at the waves rippling on the beach. It was a rare day, the sky blue, the sun shining on the mountains. There was only a small wind that sighed behind them, and ruffled their hair and clothes and flicked the tips of the waves into whiteness. On the Dragon, opposite, the stags were resting. The Hill Master had taken his hinds into a high corrie, and guarded the entrance, daring any of the bachelors to entice a mate away from him. Lexie knew where the Master hid, where he thrashed his antlers in rage, as he tossed and scored the heather, and he knew too that next year there would be many fine little beasts on the Dragon. The Master was a grand stag.

'Morag MacGregor,' he said again. 'I mind a story about a lass called Morag MacGregor. Long, long ago, ye ken.' He was lapsing into broader Scots, anxious to give the visitors full value. He was well aware of the impression he was making, and pleased. It was not often that anyone accorded him such interest. At the moment he was local colour, the real thing, the oldest inhabitant, and he intended to make the most of such brief importance.

'Tell us about her,' Ellen said. James Gunn frowned wondering if the man expected some kind of tip as recognition for his story. He looked an old rogue, and people were always ready to take advantage of a stranger.

'It was long ago, ye mind,' Lexie said. 'In the Crusades, to be precise. It is a story that they tell. Morag MacGregor, she was a bonnie wee lass, and her man went away to the Crusades, and he left her in charge of the castle.

'It was a lonely place, on a high rock looking out to sea, and the days went by and the months went by, aye, and the years went by, and the Chief didna come, and the lady was very lonely. She lived with her women and they made tapestries for the walls, to shut out the draughts, ye ken.'

He glanced at them under his eyebrows to see what kind of effect he was producing, and saw that the thought of the draughts had impressed Ellen. He knew the hotel was cold in spite of the blazing fires, and that they had heating all over the houses in America.

'The lady swore that if her man was unfaithful in the lands across the sea, and did not keep true to her memory, he would never lie by her side again. She played with her little son, and she sang to him of the old battles, and she sang the ballads that the minstrels made when they wandered through the land. And then one day a minstrel came to the castle door and her ladies brought him to her and he told her how her Lord was bewitched by a bold lass with dark eyes and with a face like a woman in a dream. He would not leave her, but his men were restless and unhappy, and at last they forced him to come and now he was on his way home.'

Lexie paused, and looked up at the Dragon. He smiled at Ellen Gunn, who was listening, enthralled, picturing this woman of long ago with her grandmother's name, living in such a wild place, among men who rode off to war at the other ends of the earth and left their wives. Times, it seemed, had not changed so much.

'The Lady Morag took a cauldron and she filled it with oil and she set it in the gateway and she lit a great fire beneath it. She watched for her man and when he came riding, his plaid flying, his hair wild in the wind, and saw her, and remember-ed, she held up her son in her arms and he spurred his horse and he galloped through the gateway and the rope that she had hung there took him by the throat and he fell from his horse into the cauldron of oil. And Morag MacGregor watched him die.'

Ellen shuddered.

'What a terrible story.'

'They were terrible times, mistress,' Auld Lexie said. 'A woman had to be as fierce as a man to survive.'

'It was a dreadful punishment for unfaithfulness,' James Gunn said. 'It's as well that women don't take the same revenge now, or there'd be a great many men dying in vats of boiling oil. And women, for that matter.'

85

'They killed an unfaithful wife, and her lover too,' Lexie said. He glanced at the farm, which lay a few hundred yards away, up the side of the Blind Man, facing the Dragon. 'Would ye care to see the pigs?' He could think of no greater treat. 'The farm at Corrie Beg breeds grand beasts.'

James and Ellen Gunn looked at one another.

'Perhaps I could take some film of the farm, and also of the girl with the pet deer and the pet lamb,' James Gunn said. He was anxious to use his cine camera and hoped that he might be shown the way up the Dragon, so that he could film the rut. As if to remind him a stag called on the hillside and was answered by instant challenge.

'Ye've heard of our Jeannie,' Lexie said.

'My son read about her and saw the deer and lamb and wrote home about them,' Ellen Gunn answered. 'We have always wanted to come to Scotland, and this sounded so unusual that we thought we'd start our tour here and see for ourselves. Nelson wrote a long letter about it. His letters home are usually so short.'

'Two things in all my life that I have always wanted, and I never did,' Lexie said. His eyes looked wistfully towards the farmhouse which they were now approaching. 'Two of the most important things in a man's life. I never reared a pig. And I never had a son. Ye are very fortunate.' He sighed deeply, and Ellen tried not to smile at the order in which the old man had placed his ambitions.

'Perhaps ye'll take a picture of me with the pigs,' he said, and James Gunn was glad of the suggestion. Lexie was a character and the folk back home would be fascinated by him, and he could reward the old man with a picture of himself too. He had both cameras with him.

Ellen stopped at the top of the rise and looked back. The sea lay smooth under a mottled sky, and behind the Dragon there were other peaks rising, bare rocks scored and crossed by a thousand runnels of foaming water, the tops blue-grey, and smoky in the distance.

A large beast moved beside the sea wall, and she grabbed her husband's arm.

'James! A wild bull!'

"Tis a Highland cow, mistress,' Lexie said. 'They are bred here as cattle. She is not as fierce as she looks, though it is not wise to go too near when she has a calf with her.'

The huge animal tossed her head. James Gunn determined to photograph her on the way back, and hoped he could get close enough to show the wide upswept horns and the long rusty brown shaggy hair and the fringe that covered her eyes. She moved away, cropping the tussocky stunted grass on the starved and boggy land that bordered the beach.

Minnie was in a small enclosure, her piglets with her. The little pigs, wildly curious, ran up to the visitors gazing bright-eyed over the fence. Ellen, who was always enchanted by the young of any breed, reached over and stroked a small head that was near to her. The piglet stamped and ran, chasing up to the sow and standing close against her, not sure about the newcomers. Lexie climbed into the run and Minnie lumbered towards him, grunting. She rubbed her head against his hand, so that he scratched her ear, and she grunted again, this time in ecstasy. She looked up as the camera whirred, but Lexie spoke to her and she relaxed and leaned against him, and the little pigs butted at his legs and hands, expecting food.

He fetched a bucket and they followed him, Minnie anxious to reach the swill first. Ellen laughed as he emptied it into the trough and the sow began to guzzle and the piglets climbed into it. One sat thoughtfully staring down at the mess, as if not sure if he were meant to eat.

'They're grand wee beasts,' Lexie said with satisfaction. 'The boar's good, too, but he's an auld devil and I'll not take ye near. He's wicked, that auld boar.'

'Do you think I could get some pictures of the deer?' James Gunn asked.

Lexie frowned.

'It will be an awful stiff climb,' he said, at last. 'The beasts go high and the Master goes highest, to keep the wee hinds from the other stags. Ye'll find it hard work. But ye can try if ye've a mind.'

They were walking towards the loch. Jeannie was in the cottage garden, looking out over the water. Rusty stood beside her, his ears wary. He could hear the noise and turmoil on the mountains and sense the excitement and the thrill that surged on the air, although he was not old enough to feel it for himself. By next year he would have his first small antlers and also have a hint of the urge that sent the bachelors trying to cut off hinds from the herds. He would not be mature enough for some years yet, nor strong enough to challenge the older and more massive stags.

Jeannie looked at him, at his wiry coat and his bright eyes, and wondered if he would grow as big as the Master, if he would show as many points on his antlers, have as deep a chest and as proud a head. She was sure that the Master was his father. She knew the big stag, had often seen him in the summer, when she climbed the shoulder of the Dragon to find Angus. The stag must be ten or twelve years old by now. He was wise and wary and in winter he stole turnips from their ground and stole hay from the ponies, and looked at her when she came near unafraid, before leaping the fence and vanishing in the trees.

Ellen, seeing the girl, thought that she looked sad. She wondered why, not knowing about Robert, nor knowing that as Jeannie listened to the stags she knew now for certain that she would have to let Rusty go, to take his chance on the hill. Perhaps he would survive, and learn to distrust men. It was a forlorn hope. He was unafraid of dogs, and he would nuzzle Angus, even when he was carrying a gun, and watch, quite unperturbed, as a hare took a running tumble, clean shot, or Jeannie practised at the target, anxious not to lose her skill.

Lexie whistled. Jeannie turned her head and saw him, and Rusty turned too. Speck, who had been curled in the long grass in the corner of the garden, bleated a welcome and ran to the gate where Rusty joined him, expectant, watching the old man delve into his pockets and take out two biscuits.

'What depraved taste for vegetarians!' Ellen said, laughing.

Jeannie came towards them shyly. She had been so long alone that it was not easy to talk to strangers, especially strangers from over the sea.

'They eat the oddest things,' she said. 'I'm sure they should not, but they both steal butter if they can get inside the kitchen and Rusty loves bread and Speck will stamp on an egg if he finds one laid by a hen in the garden instead of in the nest and they both lick up the yolk.'

Ellen loved the soft Scots lilt. She could have listened for ever to the girl's attractive low voice.

'The sheep on the hill are bandits,' Lexie grinned with sudden amusement. 'The picnickers feed them, and I saw a wee lass greeting because one of the ewes had snatched a fancy cake from her hand. Another time I saw three sheep molesting the policeman himself, who had stopped for a bite, and a drink from the burn, and who had to take his supper on to the wall, or he would have lost every scrap. They get very bold.'

'My uncle's horse likes mustard sandwiches,' James Gunn said, suddenly remembering old Warrior, who had been retired after many years at stud on his uncle's ranch. He would steal almost anything that was left near his paddock and took candy from the children, and loved cookies, and best of all loved the vast bread and beef and mustard sandwiches favoured by one of the men who worked on the ranch. He was a Scot too, only recently emigrated, a man who lived for horses, and could not find the right kind of work in England, or in Scotland, for that matter.

James Gunn filmed Jeannie playing with the animals, Fly shepherding the lamb and the deer calf, and Lexie drilling the dogs. The two collies obligingly obeyed orders and took their protégés first here, and then there, in the garden. They filmed Jeannie walking to the store with the dogs and the deer and the lamb at heel, and walking back with her purchases, while Rusty and Speck tried to rummage in the basket and find food that they could steal.

Later that week Jeannie took Ellen to the local weaving shed, where two sisters spun the wool and dyed it and made it into tweeds which held the colour of the mist and the heather and the hills and the sunset and Ellen spent so much money that Jeannie was horrified. She would not earn so much in three months, nursing.

Lexie and Angus took James Gunn up the Dragon. They climbed all day, mounting to the shoulder, but the stags had taken the hinds into safe places, and although twice heads were visible on the skyline they did not come near.

'There are beasts all round us, hiding under our noses,' Angus said. 'Not only stags, but the fox will be watching us, and there might be a wild cat, and there is a pine marten's nest and its owner will not be so far away.' He pointed to the huge ball of twigs and moss that was built in the fork of a high pine tree. 'The beasts sometimes come down and play and if ye are very still ye can glimpse them, running, or maybe washing like a cat. But they are very wary. They look like great brown weasels.'

Angus had not much accent, but it sounded strange to a man used to American speech, and James Gunn listened to the slow burr and regretted that he had not brought his tape recorder.

The Gunns spent a week in Invernay, and at the end of their time wished they could stay longer. The wild scenery attracted them, and they drove over narrow roads that had not changed since Prince Charlie stravaiged the land. Narrow roads that wound among pine woods and ended in lochs beside which hidden villages nestled. Twisting roads that climbed on to the moors, so that they drove at sunset into a land of water, where tiny lochans in the bogs reflected a reddened sky streaked with gold and massed with heavy grey cloud that stretched to the horizon. A lone fisherman flogged one of the smallest stretches of water, and then leaped from tussock to tussock to try in another place, his lean figure black against the glow of approaching night.

The day died and they drove through darkness, where Ellen

could visualise wild men lurking, and hear, in imagination, far away, the skirl of bagpipes. The sound grew louder and she sat up in her seat in fear and then relaxed as a figure showed up in the headlights, marching through the night to the bagpipes' tune, playing to quiet his own fears on the lonely road.

James Gunn drew up beside him.

'Would you like a lift?' he asked.

'Aye, so I would. Thank you very much,' the piper said, and climbed into the back of the car and sat in shy silence while Ellen tried to rouse him to talk and he answered in mono-syllables, not knowing what to say to these strangers from far away. Until she mentioned her name was Gunn and un-loosed his tongue, for Donald Gunn had been piper to his regi-ment, and he talked of the war and the places he had seen and of battles that were history now, until Ellen wondered if perhaps he were not a real man but a ghost piper, who had played at Flodden and Culloden as well as on more recent battlefields.

It was a fitting end to their stay.

Chapter Eleven

When snow masked the hills and bitter flurries were flung into Angus's face as he walked among the sheep, there was less need to guard against poachers. Now was the time to catch up with jobs left from summer, to make the cottage secure against the weather, to chop the wood that Andrew brought with him; dead wood, from the forest clearings, that made good kindling.

It was not so easy for Davie Grey to visit. The roads were often icy, and there was danger of being snowed in. His editor would not take it kindly if he were marooned in the hills for no good reason, and he could not afford to lose his job. Andrew was glad, and came whenever he was free, bringing firewood with him, or a hare that had ventured too close to the foresters' cottage. The Laird allowed them the right to shoot on their part of Nine Glens.

The deer suffered in winter. Feeding was sparse and often hidden by snow. They pawed at the ground, and hid in the woods that bordered the loch, knowing instinctively where to find shelter, and how to avoid the worst of the blizzards. Those that were bold made moonlight raids on the village gardens, taking the sprouts and turnips, and one stag thrust open a shed door with his antler, and fed on the chicken food that was stored there. Others were content to raid the hay stacks, pulling at them as they fed, scattering the ground untidily. Reluctantly Angus shot two of the bolder beasts as they were guilty of too much damage, becoming wily enough to open doors and steal winter stores of food meant for the villagers. Had Angus not shot them, an angry crofter would have taken a gun and ended the raider's life himself. There was no room for thieving in a community that could be isolated by snow and had little enough to spare for the domestic beasts.

Rusty and the lamb shared a shed where they sheltered, lying on straw. They slept together and Fly slept with them, the three beasts keeping one another warm. Jeannie found herself busier than she remembered. Angus had to take hay to the sheep, and left early each morning in order to drive up the hill. He needed to watch over them, as he could not bring them to low ground. There was no field nearby. Lambing time would be hard this year.

Jeannie had the fires to mend and the animals to feed. She had persuaded her father to build her a run and a henhouse, and added chickens to her other chores. They had lost the others in the landslide. The eggs saved her purse, and the birds would make useful additions to the menu. Now that she had recovered from her grief, and was slowly forgetting Robert she was aware that Angus found it hard to make ends meet, and that the poor feeding on the sheep hill would mean lower prices when the beasts were sold. Also there might be deaths among the ewes and lambs.

She began to take part in village activities. Life was less lonely now. There were girls her own age, girls she had known at school, and they began to visit her, and the minister's wife involved her in various activities that centred round the kirk, and Andrew often called when he had time to spare and sat watching her, talking mainly to Angus about conditions in the forest and on the Dragon, and in the Nine Glens, while Jeannie knitted, and listened and added an occasional word. She, like her father, had not very much to say. Her mother had often chided both of them, complaining that they might as well be dumb for all the conversation that she ever got from them.

Andrew enjoyed the comfort of the cottage. The forestry house was commodious but no woman ever entered it, and five men living alone did not bother about niceties. There were

93

good chairs and good beds, but it was a Spartan existence. Apart from the pin-up pictures that Jock Cameron cut from *Playboy*, and the maps of the forest, and an old calendar, there was little to brighten the place.

Jeannie had chosen pretty curtains and made cushions for the chairs, and added one or two pictures of her own to those that they had been given, pictures found in the schoolhouse, which the schoolmaster thought too frivolous for the children. He chose old masters, and hung them on the walls where they made a sombre background to the lessons.

These, which Jeannie had rescued from an old cupboard, were animal pictures, one showing a stag browsing in a sunlit buttercup studded meadow, the light from the trees dappling his coat, the other, which the schoolman had thought even more unsuitable, was a picture of Hyperion, the famous racehorse, who had sired a winner at twenty-seven years of age, and whose handsome presence spoke to the stern schoolmaster of the wickedness of gambling and the other sins of the flesh.

Angus had whitewashed the walls, and the carpets on the floor were a dull green in colour. The flowers on the curtains and the splash of red and blue and yellow in the cushions added a lighthearted air to the room. There were no flowers in winter, but Jeannie had picked beech sprays in the autumn and preserved them with glycerine, and the coppery leaves glowed against the wall.

She had bought a few cheap and colourful dishes which added a homeliness to the room that was completed by the sprawling dogs. Andrew driving through the darkness, his headlights shining on sullen naked trees and dripping dying vegetation, savoured the memory of the girl in the friendly room and knew, more than ever, that he wanted her in his own home, and that soon he would tell her of his intentions. Yet he was sure she had not forgotten Robert and did not care for him at all. He hoped that Davie Grey would stay away for the rest of the year. He had no faith in himself when it came to a clash between rivals.

Angus, watching his daughter as she worked in the house, or sat in the evening, listening and saying little, wondered if she knew how Andrew felt about her. He himself had no doubt. He was an observant man, and he had seen the expression on the forester's face when he thought he was unobserved. Andrew would make a good son-in-law and a kind husband. He wished the lass would notice what was happening under her nose. Perhaps when the spring came . . .

But spring only brought problems as snow fell and thawed and fell again, and Angus, digging out the sheep which Star found buried, slipped into a ditch and broke his ankle. He lay in pain, trying to extricate himself from the snow, and sent Tess to fetch Jeannie.

Luckily Andrew was with her, having called on his way to the store to buy a new axe, and between them they managed to bring Angus down the steep hillside, every step an agony. The doctor, used to this kind of emergency, drove him to the hospital and brought him back to lie and fume and worry about the jobs that Jeannie had to do. It was not woman's work, there on the hill, carting hay to the sheep and watching over them, and making sure that all were safe.

Lexie, hearing of Angus's accident, came daily, and dragged the hay himself, and took Star and looked over half the flock. Andrew chopped the wood and helped whenever he was free, but even so Angus knew his daughter had too much to do, what with the house and the cooking, and waiting on him, and the beasts to feed and the chickens and the sheep. He fretted and raged inwardly and developed a sour tongue, and cursed himself for his own surliness.

He tried to walk too soon, and the ankle swelled, so that once more he found himself useless. The weeks sped past, and the snow vanished, and March blustered and April came and went, and in May Jeannie spent her days and half her nights on the lambing hill, and Lexie took watch and watch with her, and together they kept away the foxes. It was hard work and cold work. Once the Vet had to come and cut a ewe and release a cross-born lamb that had jammed without hope of a normal birth. Jeannie took the lamb to the cottage and brought the ewe to the paddock to watch her, in case the cut that the Vet had made festered, but all was well.

Another ewe, unused to motherhood, refused to feed her lamb and in spite of Lexie's guile and Jeannie's coaxing the little beast was left alone. The mother had no feeling for it, no need of it, no desire to cherish or to foster it.

'I can't do a thing with her,' Jeannie said, telling Angus as they sat together over a pot of tea. Lexie was out in the field and she had come to get warm and fill a bottle for the neglected nursling.

'Put her in the lambing pen with the lamb and Fly,' Angus said. 'Tell Fly to chase the lamb. Say "chase it then," Fly knows what to do.'

'You can't mean it,' Jeannie said.

'I do mean it.' Angus looked at his daughter's disbelieving face. 'I thought you'd seen me do it before. Go out and watch. Fly will teach you something about animals, unless I am very much mistaken.'

Lexie was at the far end of the field, fetching a lamb that had been over-inquisitive, and had jammed its small body in the cleft of a twisted tree trunk. He was having a struggle to release it. Jeannie sent Fly to single the ewe. The lamb followed, uncertain and forlorn. Inside the pen the ewe dropped her head and began to feed. The lamb went to her, but she butted it away. It bleated.

'Chase it then,' Jeannie said.

Fly went up to the lamb and barked. Terrified, it bleated again and ran, Fly chasing after it, snarling. Jeannie was horrified, and about to call her off, when the lamb cried out once more.

The ewe's head went up and she saw Fly approach the lamb, growling viciously, and heard the instant agonised plaint. She rushed across the pen and caught the sheepdog with her hard skull, butting Fly backwards, tail over head, so that she tumbled to her feet and stood up, tongue lolling, mouth a-grin.

The ewe had gone to the lamb and was nuzzling him. He put his nose to her and she licked his face, and then stood quitely as he sucked, his small tail wagging in frenzy. She nosed him again, and then, when he had fed, curled on the ground and he leaned against her, his small face blissful.

'So ye have learned an auld shepherd's trick, lass,' Lexie said. He patted Fly.

'Good lass. Ye're a clever wee bitch and there's no getting away from that.'

His own dogs, lying beyond the wall, waiting, watched jealously, and he went to them and petted them.

'And ye're clever beasties too,' he said and three tails thumped the ground in blithe agreement.

Jeannie enjoyed working with the lambs. She had helped before, but never taken charge, and she found there was much to learn. Angus had no time for modern methods that dipped the sheep and inoculated the sheep and left the sheep alone, looking them over occasionally to see that all was well. There was more to shepherding than that. His beasts would not be tick ridden or maggot infested, nor would they suffer over much from fluke. Normally they fetched good prices when he sold them, but this year bad luck had dogged him and prices would be down. The grazing was very poor. Jeannie hated the lambing sales and the lorry that came and fetched the small creatures away, and the constant bleating of the ewes, bereft of their lambs. It was something she never grew used to.

'Ye need a rest, Jeannie,' Lexie said one morning, looking at her as she bent to free a leg from a tangle of thorny twig that was caught in the fleece. Fly had brought the ewe to her a moment before. The lass was thinner than ever, and her eyes were weary and it was no job for her, Lexie thought. 'Ye need a day off.'

'Where would I go?' Jeannie asked. 'I'd rather be here with the sheep. Dad can't manage on his own. He'd be walking up the Blind Man on that ankle, and it is not so strong as yet.'

'He is a stubborn man,' Lexie agreed. 'But I can watch the sheep. Young Andrew has the day off tomorrow and he told me he was going to drive into Glasgow and visit the big stores. Why not go with him?'

'I don't need to shop,' Jeannie said, and Lexie shook his head in irritation. As obstinate as her dad, and he was bad enough in all conscience. Lexie stumped off home, his dogs followed him.

Jeannie spent the day alone on the hill. It was a warm day, out of the wind, and the sheep were quiet. No need for more than a brief glance at each of them, and her work was soon done. She had brought Rusty with her, but left Speck behind. He was growing too big and irritable to bring on these excursions. The deer calf was losing his dappled coat and tiny lumps above his ears showed where the new horn was growing, but he was still lively and affectionate. He nuzzled her while she ate her lunch, and put his head against her hands, wanting the cool skin against the hot swelling that sometimes made him shake his head in puzzlement.

Across the loch the Dragon showed the faint green of new growing bracken on the scorched slopes and the waterfall was an ever present reminder of the night of terror that she had spent on the mountain. The eagle soared lazily in widening circles, dark against the blue.

He had young and the foxes had young, and soon the hinds on the mountain would drop their calves. There were hens brooding duck and grouse chicks as well as their own in the hen run.

Fly barked a swift warning, and ran.

Jeannie turned her head and saw the dog fox and jumped to action. She always carried the gun, although she had not needed it before. She called to Fly, but the bitch was protecting her sheep, and she did not pause. She ran at the fox, and he, seeing her for the first time, closed with her, so that in a moment a rolling fighting ball, rust red, and black and white, was inextricably mixed, and Jeannie dared not shoot.

She sent the pointer to join the bitch, and Rusty, always

eager, raced after them, Jeannie calling him back in vain. Fly leaped away, the fox after her, but Mac caught the beast's hind leg in his teeth and at once the intruder turned savage with frustration. The scent of lamb was strong in his nostrils and he had four cubs as well as his mate to feed. Last night he had found three mice and a baby hare and that would not keep starvation from them. He wanted a lamb, and he meant to have it.

Tess caught him on the shoulder, and Fly came back to harry his flanks. He ran from them, and turned, again at bay, and Rusty, coming up with them, and knowing from the din that the intruder was unwanted, turned his rump and kicked out and up and the dog fox fell, and rolled, and Tess came at him again.

He had had enough. He tore himself away, one leg dragging, and jumped the low wall as Jeannie fired. He was lucky. He was over the wall and in the ditch, slipping into a drain, where he laid low to recover his breath. Jeannie had no more time to spare for him. She doubted if he would return after such rough treatment. Fly had a torn and bleeding ear, hanging loose from her head, and Tess had a bitten shoulder and Mac three bites on his head and another on his hind leg, that looked as if it had been bitten through. Rusty had a bite on his rump. The fox must have been quicker than the calf, and used his teeth first. She dared not leave until she was sure that he had gone, and when she saw Andrew's Land-Rover stop outside the cottage door she stood on the wall and waved violently, delighted to see him.

Andrew came running, eager to greet her, but the words on his lips died away as she pointed to the dogs.

'The fox is in the ditch somewhere,' she said.

Andrew took the gun.

'I'll find him if he's there,' he promised, and watched her go down the hillside, the dogs limping beside her. The Vet would have a good hour's work when he came.

The fox slipped out of hiding when the smell of dog had gone. He was too badly bitten to return to find food, and

Andrew saw the rusty red body slide through the bracken and stilled it for ever, making the sheep safe for the while at least.

He found Jeannie busy washing the dogs' bites, having asked the Vet if he could call. It would be too difficult to take all the dogs and the deer as well to the surgery to receive attention. Angus was bathing Mac, who was the worst hurt of the three. Fly, having had her ear washed clean, was licking Tess's injuries.

'That ear will need stitching,' Andrew said.

He looked at Jeannie. He never seemed to find time to speak to her these days, and he had particularly wanted to talk to her when she was alone. He had brought her a gift from town, one that he thought would please her. He had seen it advertised, and changed his mind about his visit to Glasgow. It was in the Land-Rover now, and he had to get back, as although it was his day off, he had promised to cook the evening meal for the five of them.

He brought in a basket.

'I've a present for you, Jeannie,' he said awkwardly. 'I can't stay . . . I have to get back to make a meal for us all.'

Jeannie looked up at him, only half her mind on what he had said. The dogs' bites were bad and Mac's was so deep that she was afraid the leg might be permanently damaged. She took the basket and put it on the table.

'Thank you, Andrew,' she said. 'I'll open it later . . . it's very good of you to think of me,' she added, feeling something more needed to be said, but wishing that he would go so that she could concentrate on the dogs' injuries. She would be badly handicapped if the sheepdogs were unable to work. They were vital to bring sheep in need of attention to her and they were also essential when she was looking for lambs which had strayed. The little beasts might fall in one of the many gullies, or catch in a tangle of bramble or wire, or slip into the burn and be unable to climb out again. They could jump most obstacles, were adept at squeezing under fences, and constantly lively and alert and mischievous.

The Vet arrived and took one look at the dogs.

'What on earth were they doing? Eating one another?' he enquired, his voice caustic.

'A fox came into the lamb field,' Jeannie said.

'A fox? They drove him off, I hope, after all that,' the Vet said, busy with his syringe. They would need antibiotics to counteract infection.

'I shot him,' Andrew said, putting his head round the door, having started to drive away and then remembered the gun. He set it in the corner. 'It is unloaded. You won't have any more trouble with that beast.'

'Good,' the Vet said. He began to stitch Fly's ear, and she sat patiently. 'Ye're a remarkable bitch, Fly. Did ye know that then?' Fly wagged her tail gently. She knew he was trying to help her and she was never one to fuss.

Andrew hesitated, looking at the basket. He went. Jeannie heard the Land-Rover drive away again, and bent to stroke Mac, who was whimpering. He hated injections.

A strange noise sounded in the room.

Mac pricked his ears, Fly barked, Tess lifted her head, eyes wide and astonished. Startled, Jeannie looked behind her. It had been the oddest sound.

'It sounds like a cat,' Angus said.

'It can't be. They never come near because of the dogs.' Jeannie was positive.

The sound came again, a weary and plaintive note. Fly ran to the basket and nosed it.

Jeannie looked at it, and opened it. A dark head lifted, a tiny black paw reached towards her, and a small imperious voice wailed again.

'What in the world?' Angus said.

'It is a Siamese kitten.' Jeannie could not believe her eyes. She looked down at the minute creature that lay there, its blue eyes watching her, its body thin and beautiful and elegant. 'Andrew must be mad . . . with all these dogs . . .'

'He'll settle,' the Vet said. He put out a finger and rubbed

101

the pointed ears and a deep incredible purr answered him. 'He's no fear at all, the wee thing. Ye'd better find out if he's had his injections.'

'Where did he get him from?' Angus asked.

'There's only one place anywhere near that you can buy those, and I know the breeder,' the Vet said. 'That kitten's an aristocrat, and very well bred, I can tell ye. He must have cost Andrew more than a month's pay. Ye don't find these wee beasties growing on trees.'

'The man's daft,' Jeannie repeated.

'The kitten will be mad if ye don't feed him,' the Vet observed. He put his instruments away in his bag. 'That bite of Mac's is nasty, but it won't lame him. It's just a flesh wound. And none of the others need more than the usual care. You were very lucky. I'll look in tomorrow. I'm to test the cattle at the Cameron farm, so I may as well save you a journey to my house. It'll cost you no more. And find out if that wee beastie has had his injections. Ye don't want to lose him with feline enteritis. Feed him on mince meat mixed with brown bread, and cornflakes and milk, and give him some vitamin A drops on his feed. He'll eat fish and I'm very sure that Lexie will take care of that for ye. He'll grow into a fine cat. And he'll give ye a lot of pleasure.'

'I can't keep him,' Jeannie said, when the Vet had gone.

'And ye can't give him back. Lass, lass, can ye not see that Andrew is crazy about ye?' Angus had not meant to say it, but the words were out and it was too late. Jeannie stared at him.

Without a word she lifted the kitten and went out into the kitchen, holding it against her face, listening to the soft purr that throbbed in its small body. She closed the window and the door and found milk and cornflakes, and put the kitten to feed.

Her father came into the kitchen.

'There was a message in that basket,' he said. 'He has had his injections, and he has been brought up with dogs and does

102

not mind them. And there is also his pedigree. A fine impressive thing it is, with all his parents and his grandparents and his great-grandparents. His name is "Perrivale of Dragon's Dene".'

'His name is Kenzie,' Jeannie said. 'Since Andrew gave him to me he must be named after him.'

She lifted the kitten and took him into the living-room and sat with him on her lap, so that the dogs might get used to the newcomer. Kenzie did not move as one head after another sniffed at him, and Jeannie patted each one to make sure there was no jealousy. He soon tired of them and settled down and curled his paws over his nose and went to sleep. All through that evening Jeannie and Angus were aware of his throbbing purr.

When night came Jeannie found a box and lined it with a piece of old blanket.

'He'd better sleep upstairs,' she said.

'He'll need a box of earth.' Angus went to find a box and filled it and brought it to her. 'He ought to have a place of his own.'

'He will,' Jeannie said. 'He can sleep in the tiny room beside mine. It is quite empty. We can't put him with the dogs. He might get hurt or trodden on.'

She put the kitten in his bed, and looked down at him.

'A whole month's pay,' she said. 'Kenzie. The man's a fool.'

Kenzie did not answer. His eyes were shut and his small body relaxed. He lay as if dead. Jeannie went to her own bed and watched the moon, bewildered by her thoughts. She was fond enough in a way of Andrew, but she had not forgotten Robert . . . and it was too soon to change. She sighed, and her sigh was echoed by a voice beside her bed.

She looked down to see Kenzie mountaineering, climbing up the candlewick spread. His hard paws padded across her body, and he curled beneath her chin. He was not sleeping alone when there was a chance of warmth and company. Jeannie took him back to his room and shut the door, but the urgent wail grew louder and angrier and at last she laughed and gave in.

'Kenzie, you're going to be a handful,' she said. But Kenzie had had his own way and he did not deign to answer.

Chapter Twelve

Kenzie proved to have more effect on the household than all the other animals put together. His imperious voice summoned Jeannie to make his meals. If she did not come at once his cries made Fly uneasy, and she went to bring her mistress to attend to her obvious duty. The kitten was hungry.

He was also destructive, and he resented punishment. Angus tapped his paws, and spoke angrily whenever the little beast savaged the chairs or clambered up the curtains, but Kenzie had no intention of becoming obedient. He was safe at the top of the window on the rail and there he would stay until Jeannie climbed on a chair and lifted him down.

He did not stray far from the house. The outdoor world was strange and he was cautious. The ponies were huge and he eyed them with respect and kept his distance, nor did he venture near the chicken house, to Jeannie's relief. She was afraid he might clamber over the wire and make mischief among the chicks. Although small, his claws were sharp.

He enjoyed tunnelling in newspaper, and Angus, every night, put the *Evening News* down on the floor so that the kitten could crawl under it. There he lurked, ready to pounce on a waving finger, a length of string, or a dog's tail. Only Fly was patient at such cavalier treatment. The other dogs growled a warning which the kitten obeyed. He was far from stupid.

When the paper tunnel game palled, he turned the sheets into confetti, biting and tearing and spitting out the fragments, capable of making the most incredible mess. Jeannie never

105

allowed this part of the game to continue for long. It took too much time to make the room tidy again.

He discovered Rusty one bright sunny day when the deer calf jumped the paddock fence and came up to the cottage. He could clear an eight foot high wall with ease and Angus had often seen him looking up at the Dragon, as if able to see the heads among the trees that showed where his kind were lurking. He did not think that the choice would be theirs in the end. One night Rusty would leave them of his own accord. It was as well that Jeannie had Kenzie to care for. Perhaps she would not fret, although she seemed to have room and to spare for all the beasts about the place, even the stupidest of the ewes, and the lamb that had been reared with Rusty and that was now a yearling ram and developing a fine temper.

'He'll be no use for breeding,' Lexie said. 'He doesn't know that he's a sheep at all. He's maybe a dog, or a deer, or maybe he thinks he's a hen. He's daft enough. Have ye seen him with the ewe in the paddock?'

Jeannie went to look. The ewe was lying with her lamb and Speck, whose name now seemed absurd, was eyeing her thoughtfully. He went towards her and nosed both her and the lamb, and looked at them, puzzled. Mac came into the paddock, and Speck ran to him and chased him and Mac turned at bay, and the two of them began an absurd game of catch as catch can, tearing round the grass, and ending in the pair of them standing, head pushing against head, as the ram tried to thrust the dog off his feet.

Kenzie wailed.

Jeannie turned to see him flying towards her, tail erect, with Rusty in pursuit, apparently intent on catching the kitten. Kenzie reached her and began to claw his way up her leg, and she lifted him hastily. He was unaware of the pain his methods of seeking sanctuary caused.

Rusty did not like the kitten. He did not like to see Jeannie fondle the newcomer, and he lowered his head and charged her, butting with such force that she would have overbalanced if Lexie had not caught her.

106

'Hey, hey,' he said, and took the deer calf by the ears and shook his head gently. 'Ye wicked wee beast. That will not do.'

Rusty turned and left them. He walked to the end of the paddock and began to browse on the new grass, his rump towards them.

'He's jealous,' Jeannie said. She sighed. 'Animals are as bad as people . . . or people as animals. I don't know which. Come on, Kenzie. I'd better take you in and try and make friends again'. The kitten was terrified, his claws anchored painfully in her shoulder.

'Rusty's not going to be easy when his antlers grow,' Lexie said. 'I do not think we can keep him here when he's a real staggie.'

'I know that,' Jeannie said. She did not want to consider it. She had saved Rusty from death and had reared him, and he was her problem. She put the kitten indoors and took a handful of hay and went back to make amends. Rusty glanced at her, and she spoke to him. He considered her for a moment and then rubbed his head against her arm and accepted the hay and dipped his minute new budding horns into her cool hands.

'Ye're a silly wee beast,' Jeannie said, and patted him and left him to bask in the sun, eyes half closed looking up at the mountain opposite.

Davie Grey came back at the end of May. He admired the kitten and played with it.

'Where did this beastie come from?' he asked.

'Andrew gave him to me. That's why he's called Kenzie,' Jeannie answered.

After that, whenever Davie called, he brought her a small gift. A glossy magazine, a plant in a pot for the sill in the living-room, a box of bedding pansies to brighten the garden. Andrew McKenzie, becoming aware of this, called in whenever he came by, unobtrusively feeding the hens or taking the bottle to the two new orphan twin lambs now in the shed, or helping Jeannie with the sheep. He wished the reporter would stay away. The forester did not know how Jeannie felt about him

107

or what she thought, and he did not want to put her feelings to the test. If he said nothing she could not send him away. If he spoke out she might say no, and then he could have nothing more to do with her.

'I ought to go back to work,' Jeannie said one day when the doctor called to look at Angus's ankle, which was still troubling him. He could not yet do a full day's work and he was increasingly worried, lest the Laird found that a keeper who was unable to fulfill all his duties was too much of a drawback, and sacked him and employed a younger man. Between them, Lexie and Andrew and Jeannie did much of his work, but they could not watch for poachers, and the summer nights were coming, and the long summer days when the men from towns took to the hills and brought their guns and took toll of the deer and the birds on the Dragon.

'Your father can't do without you,' the doctor said brusquely. 'You're more use to him here than wearing yourself with nursing. Besides, I am not sure that your own leg would stand up to the long hours without rest. You can take your time here. But not on the wards with the sisters chivvying you and most hospitals short staffed and the girls tearing round like daft things. It's getting worse and worse.'

'That's why I thought I ought to go back,' Jeannie said. 'After all, I am fully trained.'

'If you've time to make it, I'd be glad of a cup of coffee,' the doctor said. 'I haven't had a drink this morning, and this is my last visit before lunch.'

'I'll away and look over the sheep myself,' Angus said. 'There's a lot to do.' The door shut behind him.

'Do you want to get away, or are you bothered about money?' the doctor asked. He believed in sharing his patients' worries. It was sometimes easier to treat them then. Lack of money could make a woman as ill as a physical disease, if she were hard pressed to make ends meet, and many people today were, with high prices, and low wages, up here at the back of beyond. Low enough for him too in all conscience. The doctor pushed the thought irritably away.

108

'Dad can't keep both of us,' Jeannie said. 'It's little enough he earns and not so much to come from the lambing sales this year. If I go away he could retire. It's too hard for a man of his age.'

'If he retires he'll die of boredom inside ten weeks. I've seen it happen too often. Don't encourage him to think he's old, Jeannie. That ankle will strengthen. It takes time. But if you're worried about money and have the time to spare I could do with a nurse to help me at surgery times, and there are two new babies in the village and the district nurse is hard pressed. They could pay you to come in and help for a few hours with bathing the bairns. But you'll be awful busy.'

'If I can only earn a little . . .' Jeannie was positive. The doctor drank his coffee, and stretched and yawned. 'You could help in the school, too. There's no one there to bandage the bairns when they cut themselves or to help if they feel sick. And the schoolhouse is close enough for one of the lads to come for you if you're needed. The committee could pay a retainer. It won't be much, but it will help.'

Later that day she told Angus, and he looked at her from under his eyebrows.

'Ye should have asked for some dress money,' he said. 'I didn't think . . .'

'It's not that. I'm wasting my training. I need to do something.' Jeannie grabbed Kenzie, who had taken advantage of their inattention and jumped on to the table, where he was investigating the milk jug with one small paw. He licked it, and discovering what the jug contained, put his head inside. When Jeannie lifted him he swore at her, and she tapped his nose.

'He's a bad tempered wee thing,' she said, but she laughed as she put him down and she took the jug into the kitchen and covered it up with a saucer. The milk would do for the beasts. 'He'll steal anything.'

'Cats never learn to respect property,' Angus said. No point in arguing with the lass. If she had made up her mind to work, work she must, but he wished she had less to do at home and that his own leg would not play him up. He stared at the Dragon. He had always climbed like a goat, without effort, and it angered him to find that he had to rest every few hundred yards because of the pain in his foot. He began to practise the exercises the hospital had given him to help to strengthen the weakened muscles.

Chapter Thirteen

It was Lexie who brought news of strangers on the Dragon. The dogs had found the remains of a gralloched deer, carefully buried by the men responsible, but dug up again by hungry foxes. The poachers had gutted the carcass under the trees where the earth was soft, but not dug deep enough. He thought that only one beast had been killed.

Angus cursed.

He had been afraid all summer, and rightly afraid, and he was also sure that word had spread that he was not able to haunt the slopes as in previous years. He took his gun and cleaned it, his mouth grim. He would have to yield to a younger man. He could not even run.

At one time men only came when the nights were dark, but now they might come at full moon, if they were reckless. They could see more easily, although they could also be seen.

The stags had gone to high ground. Often Angus saw a group of them, black against the skyline. The hinds were lower down, on the breeding slopes, and there were calves among them. The herd was not yet recovered from the damage inflicted upon it by the fire. There were so few beasts.

Angus sighed. In many places foresters and keepers were at war. The deer damaged the new growth in the plantations, and the stags, when their antlers were grown, thrashed and rubbed at the trees to remove the tatters of velvet, and, in the rutting season, they thrust against the bark, savage with pent energy. But here he had won the foresters to his way of thinking and there was cover on the slopes for the beasts, and strong

111

fences protected the new plantations. Perhaps the foresters would help him watch. Certainly Andrew would.

Lexie, prowling at midnight, saw a van draw up and men clamber up the hill. They did not carry guns, but they moved furtively, as if afraid of being seen. They were aware of the wind, and climbed skilfully, clambering above the hinds that lay on the slopes. The wind was blowing up the Dragon from the sea.

Lexie could move like a fox on the hunt for food. He could walk as softly as a cat, and he knew how to freeze against the tree trunks, how to avoid casting a shadow, how to be invisible as the deer themselves. He kept within hearing, and when the strangers stopped to rest, and to talk in low voices, he moved to the shelter of a bush that guarded them and crouched to listen.

'Thursday night,' one of the men said.

'And I want at least six beasts,' another added. 'Venison's fetching a good price on the market.'

'Good job the keeper hurt his leg. Might have been planned for us,' another man said. 'He's rarely on the hill these nights.'

'They'll get a younger man after this,' a voice observed.

'With a wife to keep him warm. The younger men don't walk the hills like the old men,' the first speaker said. Somebody laughed.

Lexie waited until they had gone. Thursday night. The day after tomorrow. There was a small moon, lying on its back, thin and new and without much light, but men these days used vans and were bold and flooded the hill with their headlights and dazzled the beasts and shot fast. He must warn Angus.

Angus was tired and he was worried. Rusty was irritable. His new horns were grown though not yet completely clean and he was using them, mainly on the ram, who had to be moved to an indoor stable for the time being, as Rusty could jump every fence in the place, and did when he chose, chivvying the dogs and occasionally butting Jeannie when she had Kenzie with her. The calf hated the cat. He was increasingly jealous

112

of any animal that Jeannie petted, and even Fly became a victim of his anger, and was butted by his antlers. When the velvet was completely shed he would be an even bigger problem.

And Angus's ankle was painful. At night, after a day spent among the sheep, or climbing the Dragon, it throbbed and ached and he was glad to rest. He knew he would have to give up his job as keeper soon. They needed an active man. But he also needed the money. No one could save on a keeper's wage, and there was little enough from the sheep, and the pension the Government allowed a man was not due to him for several years yet. He was only fifty-eight. It was not old. But it was too old for an outdoor job that involved miles of walking, and him as lame as a sheep with footrot. He vented his anger on Jeannie, who turned more and more to Davie Grey for companionship.

Andrew was a serious man, and as silent as her father, but Davie had a quick tongue and made her laugh, and told her ridiculous stories about his work. About the woman who came in to the office every day with a different news story; she saw murders and she saw ghosts and she saw fairies. She heard banshee screams in the night, and saw men marching down lonely glens, and she hated the MacDonalds because her name was Campbell, and she invented modern MacDonald atrocities.

He had a fund of absurdities and an imagination that ran away with him so that he embroidered and embellished until it sounded as good as any novel. He wanted to write a great book, a book that would sell all over the world and make him famous and make him rich.

'And then I'll marry you and dress you like a queen and we'll have a big yacht and travel the world and eat caviar every day and three times a day on Sundays,' he said, laughing at her.

'What would I do with my beasts?' she asked him. It was hard to think of living in a place where she could not keep them. She had missed the dogs, and the wild life on the hill, when she was working in the hospital, and always took time off to stroke any cat that she met on her way from the nurses' home to her work, and to talk to any dog that wagged his

113

tail at her. She had grown up surrounded by beasts. A world without them seemed sterile and unreal. The city, to her, seemed cold and unfriendly, a giant concrete zoo where men and women lived in cages, some of them comfortable cages, no doubt, but still cages, and people exercised on hard pavements and took a bus ride if they wished to see a tree.

'I couldn't live in a city,' she said.

'You wouldn't have to.' Davie was ebullient. He was sitting on the low garden wall beside her, and he tickled her nose with a dandelion clock. 'We'll be rich. You'll have a home in every country in the world and you can keep lions and tigers and cheetahs and panthers, and walk on roses and breathe scented air from all the flowers in your garden. And have six children all as beautiful as you.'

'Och, ye're daft,' Jeannie said.

For all that, Davie was fun and she enjoyed his visits. He brought her flowers and he brought her chocolates, and he brought Angus magazines that he thought would interest him. About car maintenance and sheep management, and about the countryside.

Davie laughed at Angus and teased him and made him talk. The keeper was an unusual man, unlike many of those whom the reporter met in his own world. Only Andrew failed to respond to Davie's charm, and sat surly and unresponsive, watching Jeannie's eyes light with laughter as she responded to Davie's quicksilver manner. The man's a clown and fool, Andrew thought sourly, but he continued to visit, for all that.

Angus worried because he liked Andrew and he liked Davie too. The reporter was good for Jeannie, but the keeper doubted if he would make a good husband, it was hard for a man with a lass to look after. He wished her mother were alive.

He was in a mood of black depression when Lexie came to him with news of the raid planned on the hill. That morning Rusty had jumped the paddock fence and chased a child up the village street, and the lad's father had threatened to take his gun and shoot the beast. It was not safe, so near to houses and bairns. If only they had not been driven off the Dragon.

114

The deer could roam in the trees up there, and they could keep an eye on him. Here . . . Angus shrugged. He would have to make a decision of some kind. Rusty would soon have small spearlike antlers to add to the danger of his games. He was becoming increasingly rougher as they grew.

'A raid on the hill?' Angus looked at Lexie. It was the last straw. 'How many men?'

'There were at least five of them and a driver,' Lexie said. 'Ye'll need help. Andrew will come with ye, and the policeman, and I can still carry a gun, and there are your dogs and my dogs. Rap is a good wee beast when it comes to a scrap. Mind how he drove off that man on the Dragon last year?'

Angus nodded. Rap had scented the man and chased him, snarling so fiercely that the raider had driven away fast on his motorbike, only too glad to escape from such an animal. He had been tying a loose shoelace when the dog found him, and had not even stopped to pick up his gun. Angus took it and handed it over to the police.

'There ought to be at least six of us,' he said. 'I'll have a word with Andrew, and ask the Laird if he can spare three men. Maybe the police from the town will help us. This is large scale poaching, not like the old days, when you had one man on his own, or two at most, and one beast dead.'

The Laird could spare three men and he could come himself. He might be over seventy but he could stalk on the hill as well as any man, and this was a ploy after his own heart. He prepared for it, whistling happily as he cleaned his rifle. No need to shoot, but it was best to be prepared. Nobody knew what kind of men came to the hills these days. It reminded him of the war. He enjoyed the taste of danger. Men lived too tame an existence. He only hoped they would catch the fellows red-handed.

Lexie led them to the slope above the hind herd. The hinds were couched in grass and bracken, the calves beside them. It was late August. Soon the stags would be among them, gathering their harems, but now they were alone, and peaceful, cropping by day, always watchful for danger, which came from

115

the foxes and the wild cats, but had not yet come from man. The Laird only culled the weaker beasts and allowed the deer to breed. The Dragon was understocked, and he was not a man with a bloodlust.

The wind whined in the pine trees. It blew from the herd to the men, so that their scent was unnoticed. So long as the wind did not veer the hinds would remain unperturbed. The Laird looked down the mountain. It was dark, but the faint light of the moon showed up the trees and glinted on the water, and revealed the eyes of all the watching beasts, and an owl that blundered out of a tree calling to his mate.

It was uncanny, waiting. The minutes crept by. A splash sounded from the loch as a fish leaped in the moonlight. The Laird eased his knee. It was stiff and aching. He hoped the raiders would come. He'd like to have them up before him on the bench. He'd teach them a lesson.

The leaves rustled faintly as a small animal scuttled for safety. Mac growled softly and was silenced by a hand on his nose. Both Angus and Lexie had brought their dogs, and all the animals knew the need for quiet. No one would have guessed that they lay in the bushes with their masters. On the road below the van turned on to the forestry track. It made surprisingly little noise. Angus shifted his position, easing his aching foot. The policeman had a thistle pressing against his knee. No matter how he moved, it remained there. He wished they would hurry. There was a police car hidden among the trees just off the ride, and he had a torch to flash to the driver. Three other men were hidden close by. A police van waited, out of sight, in a clearing just off the road beside the loch far below. The Laird had mustered all the help he could.

Waiting was the worst part, Andrew thought. He wanted action, wanted to ease cramped legs, to lash out. It would help the sullen anger that was growing inside him as he watched Jeannie's face lighten with laughter when Davie began to fool.

The old hind was on her feet, uneasy. She could hear the van. She had not heeded it at first. Cars often passed on the lochside road, their engines plainly audible. There was no threat

116

from them. This one was coming closer. Her ears moved. She was standing in a clearing and the bulk of her body and the outline of her head were plain, black against the greyer shades of night. Another hind roused, and nosed her calf.

The herd was alert, but as yet unworried. The van came round the corner, and the headlights flashed on full, dazzling the beasts. They ran, in blind panic, pell-mell, senseless, not knowing how to escape from the sudden terrifying glare, which none of them, not even the old hind, had ever seen before.

As the beasts bolted, one of the policemen moved forward and shouted, too late to prevent the shot that dropped a hind at the edge of the herd. She fell, injured, but not dead. Her legs thrashed in agony.

Angus yelled.

'Put out those lights. Shoot again and I'll shoot the lot of ye.'

One of the men swore, his voice vicious, and loosed a shot towards the keeper. The policeman flashed his torch, and a voice called from the trees.

'You're surrounded . . . Drop your guns.'

A man turned and fired again, and the Laird, who was standing in the best position, shot out the headlights of the van. Everyone was blinded by the sudden darkness. Angus heard the deer bolt for safety, hooves drumming.

'Ye haven't a chance,' the Laird called. 'There are men all round ye.'

'He's bluffing,' one of the poachers said. 'Into the van lads.'

The police car, which had been waiting beyond the curve of the rough forestry road, drove forward, headlights blazing. Two men were climbing into the van, a third stood at the door, and beyond them were two more, slipping away among the trees.

'Put down your guns,' Angus said again. 'I have ye covered.'

A shot sounded behind them. Heads turned. One of the policemen jumped towards the van, and snatched a gun before the owner could use it. He covered the men in front of him.

117

They dropped their weapons, and stood, sullen and cowed.

'Guard them,' Angus said, and Mac and Tess bounded forward, snarling. Mac stood, teeth bared, and the policeman relaxed.

A second shot sounded below them, followed by a sharp bark and a human yell of pain.

'That will teach ye,' Lexie's voice said, smug with satisfaction, and the village policeman shone his torch downwards among the pines, revealing the old man walking up the hill, his gun levelled, the two poachers walking in front of him, one of them holding a handkerchief over his bitten wrist. Lexie's mongrel dog followed at their heels, snapping at their ankles, and snarling savagely. He was ready to bite again. Lexie had fired harmlessly into the air. The threat had been sufficient to cow the poachers.

The police van came up the hill and the prisoners were locked inside. Angus watched it drive away. The injured hind lay helpless. He went to her, and seeing that her wound would kill her within a day or two and that nothing more could be done, he shot her, and walked back to the Laird, his face grim. She had milk in her, and unless he could find the calf there would be another death to the poachers' account.

His leg ached and he was limping. The Laird watched him. Angus was a good keeper and he had served him well. He needed some help.

'It's time we took in a younger man for you to train to follow you,' he said, as Angus approached.

'Ye need not make it easy for me,' Angus said, glad to have the matter out in the open. 'A lame man is no use on the Dragon.'

'And a young know-nothing is no use to me,' the Laird said. 'It will take the rest of your working life to train a man to your standard. No one else knows the Dragon as you do, unless it's auld Lexie here, and his knowing is not to his credit.'

Lexie grinned. The Laird had sentenced him more than once for poaching, but they had a sly liking for one another for all that. The Laird was a fair man, and Lexie was careful.

118

He took care not to give frequent offence.

'You can share the duties,' the Laird said. 'A younger man can patrol at night and let you lie in your bed, and you can hatch out the grouse chicks for me, and train the dogs. There's not a man can train a dog like you. I spoke to Donald MacDuff at the Big House at Lochside. He has two retrievers that he wants teaching. They've been spoiled by his shooting visitors, who allowed them to run after injured birds, and have begun chasing and killing chickens. He wants them taught properly and he has no time.'

'I can do that, and welcome,' Angus said. There might be a place for him after all.

'See you charge him a proper price,' the Laird said. 'He can afford it. You'd better come up to the house for a tot, and then McKie can drive you back to the Land-Rover. There'll be no more trouble for a while, not when the newspapers hear of this.'

'A good job no one was hurt by the shooting,' Andrew McKenzie observed an hour later, as they stood by the huge old fireplace, where logs blazed brilliantly. The dogs lay by the door, Mac and Tess on the one side, and Lexie's three beasts on the other, eyeing one another covertly, well aware that there would be instant retribution if they argued with one another. Tess slept, not caring, but Mac had no eye on the other three, and the mongrel watched Mac, ready to defend himself should the other dog stir.

'They knew what was good for them,' the Laird said. 'And we proved we could shoot straight too, which would make them think twice about using guns. I've never seen any one of them about here before. They must have come from Glasgow, or even farther afield.'

'I hope that's the last of them for a while,' Angus said. He was tired. He wanted his bed, and he wanted to rest his aching leg.

'McKie can pick up that hind,' the Laird said. 'We might as well use her.'

'I wonder where the calf has gone.' Angus was morose. Rusty

was problem enough, and now he might have to add another pet deer to the menage. And he did not want to look for it.

He had no need to worry. McKie, the Laird's chauffeur, dropped them beside the Land-Rovers. As Angus walked wearily towards his he heard a forlorn bleat. Andrew looked at him.

'Go on home,' he said to the other two foresters. 'I'll join you in the morning. I'll stay with Angus now.'

The foresters drove away, and the two men walked towards the sound. The calf had come to find her mother, and was nosing her stiffening body, bleating forlornly. She was very small, born late, and not more than six weeks old. She was too bemused to move when the men approached her.

Andrew lifted her, and she bleated again and struggled, but he held her firmly. She would not leave her dam. She would lie beside the body, trying to wake the hind. And she would need milk. Jeannie had another chore to perform tomorrow.

'Maybe Rusty will take to the wee one, and will not be jealous,' Angus said, as Andrew took the wheel. It was good not to drive. The clutch on the Land-Rover was heavy and his ankle was throbbing. Behind them, the calf bedded down on sacking, too bewildered to struggle or complain. Angus was asleep before Andrew had driven more than five hundred yards. The younger man glanced at him in pity. It was a hard life for the old man. If only he could help him more. If only Jeannie would show some sign of liking. If only Davie Grey would keep to the city and to the type of girl who would appreciate his kind of life.

It was useless to brood. The headlights shone on the edge of the loch, and the trees at the side of the road were dark and ghostly shapes that rustled under the moon. Behind him and above him the black build of the Dragon crouched beneath the sky, and the wind that seared the slopes rattled a loose bumper on the Land-Rover, and whistled through the top of the open window.

Tess and Mac crouched at Angus's feet, and leaned against his legs, also sleepy. Andrew begun to feel that no one else was alive in the chilly night. No lamps shone in the village street, and the houses gloomed under the shadow of the Blind Man, black against the dark. Bright eyes gleamed as a cat stared towards him and then slipped off the low wall on which it was standing and hid in the grass.

Andrew drove in at the gate and parked beside the cottage. Angus roused wearily.

'Ye'd best sleep on the couch,' he said, and opened the front door, and stumped up to bed. Long after he had gone, Andrew lay in the quiet room and watched the stars slide over the sky, and listened to an owl that screamed in the tree outside, and to the soft chunking clock, and the splash of the waves on the shingle. They had left the calf in the Land-Rover. They could not introduce her to either Rusty or the ram at this time of night, nor could they leave her free. She would try to return to her mother.

If he married Jeannie, perhaps they could build a new house in one of the Nine Glens. She could keep all the beasts she liked up there, and if they were close to the road she could learn to drive, and visit her friends in the village. It would be a good life, there in the forest. It was almost dawn before he fell asleep.

Chapter Fourteen

Andrew woke early. He would have to walk most of the way back to the forestry cottage; if he were lucky he would meet one of the other men starting out for the day in the Land-Rover. He went to look at the calf. It was lying quietly, forlorn, and he guessed it needed milk.

The goat was in her own stall, in one of the sheds that Angus had erected at the top of the paddock. Neither Rusty nor the ram was to be seen. Perhaps the nanny would foster the calf with her own kid. He lifted the tiny beast, and carried her across the grass.

Nan had fostered cow calves and a Shetland pony whose mother had died during a prolonged and difficut birth. The Vet had completed the event by operation, removed the tiny exhausted foal, and in desperation, given it to the goat who always had enough milk for three kids. She accepted the little beast without fuss, mothering him until he was much bigger than she, and although no one was aware of the fact, she had often allowed Rusty to suckle when he was small.

She licked the hind calf. The small animal was starving, and went to her at once, and began to feed. Nan settled happily. Andrew watched to make sure that all was well and then closed the door, leaving the goat and her kid and the deer calf curled up together. He wrote a note for Angus and left it on the kitchen table and let himself out of the house. He did not want to make additional work for Jeannie, and did not like to raid the pantry and find food before his long walk to the fifth of the Nine Glens.

Rusty had solved Angus's problem for him during the night. Restless and irritable, he had prowled around, unable to settle. Angus had shut him in early, anxious to finish his jobs before lying in wait for the poachers, and the door was not fastened properly. Rusty, pushing and nosing against it, found that the latch had slipped, and at once he was outside in the dark. The fence was no problem. He could clear eight feet at a bound, and soon he was trotting beside the loch, his small hooves thudding on the tarmac road.

A car passed, revealing him, briefly in its headlights. He was used to cars. He was full of energy and he wanted to run. Five miles to the foot of the Dragon, and then he was climbing through the pinewoods, the needles soft under his feet; there was grass and heather, and he stopped to browse when the sun lifted over the top of the Blind Man and drenched the world with light. He had forgotten all the lessons that his mother taught him, and when Lexie saw him climbing towards the shoulder of the Dragon, and called, Rusty did not turn his head. He had his own business to attend to, and he had no desire to return to the cottage.

Freedom was exciting. He galloped through one of the rides, his nose telling him that hinds were near. This time they did not thrust him away. He was not seeking food, or mothering. Nor did he smell of dogs. He had sought solitude for days, avoiding his former companions. The hinds let him bide. There were other small stags with newly grown antlers, and he ran with them and butted against them, and he followed them when they obeyed the old hind's signal to run, but he did not know why.

There was excitement in the forest. He learned, once more, to melt among the trees, to stand, watching, when men came near, and to follow the hinds when the old beast alerted them. He played with the young deer who were born when he was born, and he watched the older stags, as they trotted along the skyline, far up on the heights, away from the hinds and their young.

There were new scents to master; scent of rabbit and hare,

of grouse and ptarmigan; the summer tang of heather and the flavour of damp bracken. He knew the sound and sight and smell of the sea, and of drying weed borne on the wind, but the odour of resin from the pine trees was unfamiliar, and there was need to learn what he could eat. He had always been fed by Angus or Jeannie. There was no bottle for him now, nor hay spread on the ground. The feeding was poor, and the deer covered large areas in their quest for fodder.

At the end of his first week on the Dragon a red setter came running up the hill. He was a town dog, a spoilt pet, untaught and undisciplined, and at the first chance of freedom from his owners, who were staying in a guest house in the village, he bolted, and spent an hour among the sheep at Corrie Beg, teasing the lambs, and chasing the ewes, until the farmer, incensed, loosed a shot over his head. Luckily for him he had never heard a gun before and the sound terrified him so that he ran, panic mad and stupid, until he reached the woods on the Dragon and began to climb the slope.

He chased a rabbit and gambolled after a hare, and sat, grinning, mouth wide and his tongue hanging, watching the birds. He barked, and heard the echo of his bark and answered it, puzzled by the sound of another dog calling to him in his own voice. The deer, hiding in deep cover, listened. He was far enough away and they had not caught his scent, but they were wary.

The setter drank from a pool, and lolloped on, anxious to explore such a fascinating world. He marked his path, nosed a mouse from under a leaf, and left it trembling with terror as it stared up at the huge beast that towered above it and breathed rankly over its minute body. He chased a small bird, and then, tail waving, ran up the centre ride.

Rusty knew dogs and was not afraid of them. Mac and Tess, Star and Fly and Lexie's three, these were his friends and with them he played tag, butted and pushed and ran in mock terror. He walked out of cover. The sentinel barked in alarm; the herd fled up the ride and vanished in the trees. The old hind, annoyed because Rusty had not followed her, ran back

124

and kicked him sharply. He did not understand. He walked towards the dog. It seemed more familiar and friendly than the grandmother, who in her anxiety to teach him safety, had just meted sharp punishment.

The dog saw the two deer and barked joyously, running towards them. The old hind vanished, but Rusty stood his ground. The setter, over excited, and eager, jumped at the young deer, and bit deep into the shoulder that was nearest to him.

The hot blood pouring from the wound terrified Rusty. He had been bitten by the fox, but then the dogs had attacked it first and he understood that the beast was an enemy. He had accepted the setter as a friend. As it turned again and leaped for his back, suddenly hot with the joy of killing and the desire to hurt and to feed, Rusty gathered his wits and ran.

He ran through the trees, towards the distant loch. He knew that there, beyond the deep water, was the cottage, and Jeannie, and safety. He knew that Fly would come to his aid, and drive off this witless beast that bothered him so much. The setter was close at his heels, barking furiously. Rusty fled down the Dragon, leaping the rocks, fear growing until it mastered him and he had no sense left. He turned once, at bay, and lowered his head, but the dog jumped to one side, and tore at an exposed flank, lacerating the flesh. The pain was more than the deer calf could bear.

He was panting as he ran, breath searing his throat, his heart racing. He dived between dark trunks, crossed the ride, and plunged downwards, hurtling over rocks that lay in his path, bounding over the burn, sliding on wet mud, finally reaching the road and running to the beach, just in time to avoid a car that sped round the bend and caught the chasing setter fair and full. The driver stopped, but it was too late. The dog was dead. Cursing, he put the body in the boot. He could not possibly have avoided the beast.

Rusty did not know that his pursuer had died. He only knew that he must reach Jeannie, and he waded into the sea, and began to swim across the water. Blood stained the waves, and salt stung the wounds, but determination drove him on. Here, where the loch was shallow and the tide was out, he had only a short swim across the water. His small head crested each wave, but his strength was lessening. He drifted with the current, knowing that he must reach shore, and that he would find help at the cottage.

Lexie had spent the day before with Jeannie, whose mind was full of the missing deer calf. She was sure that Rusty would come to harm on the Dragon, and she had begged Andrew McKenzie to drive her there every evening so that she could scan the hill through her father's spyglass, but although she had seen the hind herd, she had not seen her deer calf.

'Ye knew he would have to go,' Andrew said, when they returned from one of their unsuccessful forays.

'That doesn't make it any easier,' Jeannie said pettishly. She could not bear the thought of the calf on the mountain. He did not know how to feed in the wild and the other deer might hurt him. He was too tame, too used to men, too accustomed to having his food brought to him.

Not even Davie could cheer her, although he tried his best, and came every evening, bringing with him absurd gifts. A pencil two feet long and an inch thick, topped with a Scotsman's head with a long red nose and a saucy tartan tam o' shanter. A wooden beast that looked like a cross between a giraffe and an elephant, with a nodding head and a twisting tail; a catnip mouse for Kenzie, that the kitten licked until it was a sodden mess and then abandoned on Jeannie's clean washing; a pot of white heather.

Davie began to curse the beasts that took so much of her time and attention. He became demanding, and began to irritate her, and Andrew seeing this, was glad to wait, and to take her out to look for the calf, and to continue to help her father.

Lexie searched too. Twice he saw the calf, but Rusty had no mind for him, and did not answer when he called. The old man was sitting on a rock on the beach when he saw the calf swimming in the water. That morning he had woken with a pain in his head and a fire in his chest. He fed the dogs in a dream, and left food for the three cats, who spent the nights

126

in the woodland. They were almost wild, and no one but Lexie could come near any of them. The one-eared Tom guarded both the tabby queens, and fathered their kittens. Sometimes Lexie found the little cats and gave them away, but often they roamed wild. Three had taken to the woods, and the rest had fallen victim, when very small, to marauding foxes.

Lexie left his hut and walked slowly down the side of the Dragon. He was dizzy and sick and he needed help. He would visit the doctor and find out what was wrong. He was old, and today felt older than ever, so that time drifted in a dream, and he was not sure of the year or the date. The dogs walked beside him, and Rap butted his hand anxiously, unable to understand why his master was so slow, and reluctant to notice a wagging tail or eager head.

Lexie rested on a rock on the slope of the Dragon and watched the cars speed by below him. Once, long ago, there had been horses and carts along that road, and the only surface was mud that was dry and dusty in summer, and churned to a morass in winter. There had been an old horse, a grey, a lovely gentle beast called Mac who had pulled his father's cart, long long ago.

Momentarily, as the sun warmed him, the pain in his head and chest eased. He saw the dogs watching him, the blind dog leaning against him, and remembered that he had seen Rusty on the Dragon and he must tell Jeannie that the wee staggie was well, and lively, and living among his kin. He stood up and plodded down the last slope that led to the road. A van slowed to a stop. It was the butcher from Invernay.

'Would ye like a ride to the village, Lexie?'

'Aye, I would be glad,' Lexie said, returning to the present day world with an effort. He whistled the dogs and they jumped in with him, the blind bitch on his knee, the other two at his feet. The butcher, glancing sideways, was shocked to see how much the man had aged. He looked weary and ill. It could not be good for him to live in that dilapidated hut, miles away from anywhere.

Lexie did not want to talk. He was thankful to sit and be

driven towards his goal. The pain was back again and he remembered why he had come. The doctor did not hold a surgery until the afternoon, but he would sit on the beach beside the water and watch the waves licking the shingle, and look at the herons as they fished, and at the gulls that turned the weed to find food, and there might be seals. He left the van at the edge of the village and nodded his thanks. The cottage where Jeannie and Angus lived was quiet, and there was no sign of the lass. She would be at the store, or up on the hill with the sheep, or perhaps looking for Rusty. The tiny hind calf lay in the paddock beside the nanny goat, obviously sure that she had a new mother.

When he reached the beach the pain returned. It was difficult to breathe, impossible to think. Lexie sat, his face grey, feeling the cold of the rock seep through his clothes to his bones, feeling the breath of disaster chill on his cheeks, aware of nothing but the necessity to breathe, conscious of each movement of his lungs, each uneven beat of his thudding uneasy heart dominating every moment, blood pounding in his ears.

When Rap barked, Lexie looked up, and for a moment the pain cleared. He saw the deer calf's head, saw the small beast try to clamber from the water, and saw blood running down the smooth brown coat. He had to help, had to hurry, and he tripped and stumbled until he reached the sea and waded in, and hefted the deer.

Rusty was big and he was heavy. The old man tripped and fell, and his head hit a rock. The deer calf, exhausted, dropped beside him and the three dogs came running, the blind bitch following the scent of the other two, stumbling over unseen stones and boulders, and whimpering her distress.

Lexie did not hear. He would hear nothing in this world, ever again, and he lay on the shore, at the edge of the receding tide, and Rusty bathed him with his blood, while the bitch and the two dogs, sensing disaster, sat by their master's body and howled at the sky.

Jeannie, returning from the village store, heard them, and glanced across the beach. She saw the old man lying still and saw Rusty beside him, and she spoke to her own dogs and made them wait, and jumped over the wall, and ran, sliding and slipping on the wet rock, until she reached them. Rusty heard her voice and bleated, a forlorn sound, and struggled to his feet and went towards her. Blood matted his coat, and his legs refused to hold his weight. He fell again. Jeannie went towards him, wanting to comfort the deer, but anxious to help the old man, to lift his head, to make him move away from the wet beach. Rap would not let her near. He straddled his master's body, growling furiously, defending him with all his might against harm. Jeannie called and cajoled, but in vain. If she moved closer the dog would bite. He left her in no doubt of that.

She did not know what to do. The deer needed attention, and she was afraid that Lexie was dead. If he were alive and in need of help she would have to bring it fast. She ran along the beach and vaulted the wall, and raced back towards the store. She telephoned the Vet and telephoned the doctor.

The postmistress heard her and called to her son, and he brought his car, and went to fetch the garage owner, who would also help. But none of them could coax Rap away from his master. The mongrel had given all his love and all his loyalty to the man who befriended him, and they were not going to come and take him away.

Jeannie had a lump in her throat and tears in her eyes.

'Rap, lad, Rap, lad,' she coaxed, but the coaxing was futile. The blind bitch had come to her for comfort, and the whippet, and she fondled them both, but the mongrel would not be quietened or consoled.

'We can't waste time,' the garage owner said. 'The old man needs help.'

Boldly he walked towards him, careful to show no fear of the dog, but Rap leaped at him and bit savagely. The man stepped back, nursing a wrist that was bitten to the bone.

'There is only one way.' The village policeman had joined them. 'Jeannie, get your father's gun. We can't let the dog be. Quick, lass.'

Jeannie ran. She seemed to have been running all day, and she was out of breath when she reached the cottage. She loaded the gun and carried it back carefully, knowing that this time it was not wise to hurry. It was too easy to slip and fire the gun by accident. But she could not shoot the dog. She gave the gun to the policeman and turned her head away.

'Puir wee beastie,' the garage owner said. He lifted the dead mongrel and bent over the old man.

'He is dead already,' the policeman said. 'He hit his head as he fell. It must have killed him then.'

Jeannie went to the deer. She did not want to look at Lexie, did not want to remember that he would never call on her again, never help her with the beasts, never come in at the doorway, his white hair on end, his bright eyes smiling, pleased to see her and eager to greet her and always grateful for the little help she could give him, and for the fact that even at his age, he could be of use to her and to Angus.

The Vet's Land-Rover drew up beside the sea wall, the doctor drove up behind him. They came together over the beach, walking carefully on the treacherous weed, still wet from the receding tide. The doctor bent over the old man.

'I think he had a heart attack,' he said. He looked at the deer. 'He must have tried to help the beast. It would be the kind of thing that Lexie would do.'

It would indeed, Jeannie thought, and walked silently beside the Vet as he lifted Rusty and took him to the Land-Rover. She remembered the dogs, and called to the blind bitch and the whippet and they came after her, tails down, bewildered by the loss of their master. She could not look at Rap, who lay on the rocks, and had died because he loved his master too well.

'Ye can't help, lass,' the Vet said. 'We'll have work to do on this beastie. It looks as if he has been savaged by a fox, or maybe a dog. Those are wicked bites, and he's exhausted.'

'Will he be all right?' Jeannie asked, but the Vet did not answer. He did not know how deep the bites went and the deer might well die. Jeannie would sorrow. She was a daft wee lass, always too set on her beasts, but it was not the kind of fault that he would criticise. He sighed. People were sometimes more of a problem than the animals they brought him. He put the animals in the Land-Rover, and drove to the cottage.

Behind them, the men lifted auld Lexie, and then took the dog and put him beside his master. The garage owner needed immediate attention for his bite. There was no end to it, the doctor thought wearily as the policeman went to call an ambulance and they covered the still body and left it behind the wall. The postmistress's son remained on guard while the doctor drove the garage owner to his surgery, where he could give him attention.

'Puir beastie,' the man said, bearing no grudge.

Jeannie, sponging blood from the deer's wet coat, thought sorrowfully of the old man, and, when at last they left Rusty lying on straw, she took the blind bitch and the lame whippet into the house with her and fussed over them. They knew the pointers and the collies, and they settled at last on the rug by the fire, but they lifted their heads at every footstep, and their tails wagged feebly and then stilled when Angus came home.

'Och, lass,' was all that he could say when he heard the story. Poor auld Lexie. He'd not had much of a life, though he had seemed to enjoy it. Angus fondled the two animals, and then went to look at the deer. Rusty lay in the straw, safe among familiar people. His eyes watched Angus, and he nosed the man's hand, but made no attempt to feed.

'Lexie would have given him brandy,' Jeannie said, and then the tears she had been fighting refused to stay hidden and she ran indoors, while Angus made a drink of warm milk laced with brandy and persuaded the deer to suck from his old familiar bottle. The man was sure that the beast would die.

Chapter Fifteen

The dog had bitten an enormous gash in Rusty's shoulder, tearing away both skin and muscle. Ian Campbell, the Vet, could offer little hope. Everything depended on the animal's resistance. The wound festered, and Jeannie spent her days dressing it, bathing away the pus, while Rusty hovered in a twilight world and ignored her presence.

She was determined that he should live. Angus watched her, knowing that she had every intention of exhausting herself before she allowed the beast to die. She force-fed him with a mixture of glucose and warm milk and water, using a medicine dropper to give him a little nourishment every hour. Andrew, coming to see whether the deer was surviving, looked at her with exasperation and offered to sit up for part of the night, and help make sure that Rusty had every chance of life.

'Lass, lass,' Angus said wearily on the third evening, as she sat over her meal, scarcely bothering to taste food, 'he is only a beastie. Ye can't work miracles. It isn't fair to keep him alive. Let Ian Campbell put him down, or let me take the gun and put him out of his misery.'

'He is not going to die,' Jeannie said and she said it again when Davie came to talk to her as she knelt in the straw, bathing the wound.

'You can't spend your life like this.' Davie did not like sickness or injury. He could not bear to look at the gaping flesh. Nauseated, he went outside again, and after talking to the air, and exhorting Jeannie in vain, he rode off on his motorbike, sure that any girl who could so absorb herself in the affairs of a brute beast was not, after all, the girl for him. Jeannie did not even notice when he went.

'If he isn't better by Saturday, I will have to put him down,' the Vet said, when Thursday had come and the deer showed no improvement. He was barely alive. He swallowed the glucose mixture that Jeannie fed him, and sometimes opened his eyes and looked up at her, or at Andrew, or at Angus, who had decided he had better take a turn at nursing or his daughter would be a wraith instead of a girl. She seemed not to notice the people about her, and Davie's absence passed quite unremarked. Angus had thought that she would miss him.

Troubles, it seemed, rarely came alone. On Thursday night the village was saddened to hear that the Laird, who was old, but not so old as some, had died in his sleep, from a heart attack. He had no heir. Angus walked down to the village store to try and find out whether anyone knew who was likely to succeed to the estate, but all that was known was that the nearest relative was a cousin in London who would probably sell everything. He had his own business, and was not interested in anything north of the border.

Angus left the store and went back to the cottage. Jeannie was silent, completely absorbed by her anxiety for Rusty. She drifted restlessly from the kitchen to the shed, trying to find some small grain of comfort, some sign that the little beast was improving, that he was eager for food, that he knew her when she knelt by him and stroked the harsh fur that had lost its gloss, and tried to attract the brown eyes that stared dully at the wooden walls. Fly had returned to her old charge, and spent much of her time beside her foster child. The tiny hind was thriving, feeding from the nanny as if she were a kid and not a deer calf.

'I'm taking the dogs up the Dragon,' Angus said. 'I'll be late tonight. Is Andrew coming?'

Jeannie nodded.

'Maybe he will stay with ye until I come.'

'I don't mind being alone,' Jeannie said irritably. She wished her father would leave her to herself, and stop advising her and trying to help her. She had no need of him, or of Andrew, or anyone else. Life was bad enough without being fond of people too. She was sure that Rusty would be dead by morning. Everything that she loved died. There was a curse on her. She wished Angus would go.

Angus sighed. He would come back as soon as he could. He did not like to leave her too long on her own.

Jeannie went back to the shed. Rusty looked up at her, for the first time for two days. She bent to him and smoothed the fur on his hard little head, and caressed his ear. He leaned against her hand, responding.

She fed him with glucose and a little milk from the nanny goat, and water, and he swallowed. She called the nanny to her, and the beast came obligingly. Rusty looked up at her, old instinct guiding him, and began to suckle. Had he stayed with his mother, he would have shared her milk with her new calf, although he had long learned to browse and fend for himself.

'He'll mend,' the Vet said, coming to look through the door. 'That is a very good sign. Let the nanny stay with him. And the wee hind. Perhaps he will not be jealous of her. But, Jeannie, when he is well again, ye will have to let him go, or ye will have to geld him. He can't stay as he is. He will hurt someone with those antlers. And the villagers will not like it. He is getting a bad wee beast.'

'He can't go back,' Jeannie said. 'Someone will shoot him, or another dog will chase him. There are always campers here in the summer, and their dogs aren't trained to the country.'

The Vet nodded.

'One of them killed the duck that was breeding on the lochside,' he said. 'The drake tried to rear the young by himself, but he couldn't do it, and he lost most of the ducklings. A fox took one, and another dog killed two others. I chased him off, but it was too late. People don't care.'

People don't care.

It became the main theme of Angus's thoughts in the weeks that followed. He looked over the sheep and walked on the

Dragon, but there seemed little point in planning for the future until he knew what was to happen to the Estate. There was to be an auction later in the year. The new Laird was a cousin, with his own home and business and he did not want the place. It was too remote, too old, too unprofitable, and the cousin did not like wild places or wild beasts, and neither did his wife. There would be no more of the family up at the Castle.

In the hotel bar at night the men of the village talked of the future, but without much hope. Many of them owed their homes to the Laird and wondered uneasily if the new owner would dispossess them, or if he could raise their rents. There was little pleasure in companionship. Each man sat, brooding, and Angus took a dram of whisky more frequently, hoping to ease the troubles that beset him. Jeannie had recovered her old ways again, now that Rusty was well, but Andrew haunted them, his eyes miserable, and Angus wanted to shake the lass and knock some sense into her. She had no right to do that to the man.

'It will not be the same here, ever,' the postmaster said mournfully, late one evening. He raised his glass. 'The auction is soon, and we will know the worst.'

Angus did not answer. The hotel depressed him. It was big and cold and bleakly furnished and the bar, since Lexie died, was an unfriendly place, even though the old man's visits had been rare. He had sat there and regaled them with tales of old Scotland, and he had had a way of making the ballads come alive, and the Laird had sat opposite the old rogue and encouraged him, and the two of them had often sung together. The Laird had been a grand man. No one could replace him.

Rusty was gelded, and when autumn turned the trees to gold, and rain dripped from a sodden sky, and clouds darkened the Dragon's heights, and the roars of the stags reverberated in the hills, the little stag showed no interest, although at times he looked upwards, as if missing the herd. The small hind nuzzled against him, and he turned to her and touched her nose, and forgot his fret. His antlers would drop and might

135

never grow again, but the operation had already gentled him, so that he was a different beast, and there was no fear that he would turn in anger and gash and gore.

Time passed unbelievably slowly. There were signs of footrot among the sheep and Angus dipped the hooves of each in a solution containing chloramphenicol, and applied terromycin ointment to the worst cases. He brought one of the ewes down to the shed, as she had an additional infection, caused by a cut, and put a protective leather boot on her. She complained mournfully, disliking being alone. She would soon heal and could return to the flock. She was not used to people, and he needed Fly to guard her in case she managed to escape when he opened the shed door to treat her. Sheep were surprisingly agile and very wary. Although classed as domestic beasts they were not used to human handling, and unless men were frequently among them, allowed no one near. Sometimes a flock might learn that picnickers fed them, and become tame, asking for food, snatching it from children's hands, as they ate sandwiches on the hills, on week-end outings with their parents.

Angus wished he could move his sheep to another field. The pasture was infected and he would need to make sure that footrot did not romp through the flock. If it did, the ewes suffered, and either knelt to feed, to relieve the pain and put less weight on their hooves, or grazed, standing on three legs, holding first one hind leg in the air and then another, in an effort to gain comfort. He needed a field that had not been used for weeks, and that was impossible. The only grazing was behind the Castle. The old Laird would have let him take the sheep up there, although it was a long way to go to look them over. He could not take the liberty now. The new owner might object. If only the Laird had not died.

Jeannie was aware that her father was brooding, but she was too busy to spend time with him, and did not know how to distract him. She was occupied with the school, taking sick children home, or bandaging knees and hands cut or grazed at playtime. She helped the District Nurse, and had found three old ladies who lived by themselves, each one in a tiny white-walled cottage like a child's drawing, two windows and a front door, and geraniums in pots on the sills, and cats that sprawled across the doorsteps in the sun.

The old ladies were lonely, and Jeannie began to visit them, and then found that they could not manage their household chores. She helped with those too, and discovered their meagre pantries, too little food on the shelves.

She brought them broth and jellies, and meat, when her father brought home a hare or a rabbit. They watched for her eagerly, glad to have young life in the place, even if briefly. So few people had time for them, or cared about their rambling stories of past days when they too had been young and active, and part of the community.

Their homes belonged to the Estate and they were worried lest the new owner raise the rents. Nobody knew if he could, but all feared the worst. Change was always unwelcome, and it would not be the same to have new owners on the Dragon. Maybe city folk who only came for the shooting and brought their own guests and never came near the village.

The farmer at Corrie Beg was as gloomy as the rest of the villagers. He rented his farm from the Laird and new owners might have new ideas. It was a small farm, that only just paid its way. Maybe there was room for improvement, for new methods that would show a bigger profit, and there were always means of making a sitting tenant's life so irritating that he preferred to move. The newcomers might not be so scrupulous as the Laird's family, and they would have no interest in the history of the Estate, or people who owed their loyalty to the man who had been Head of his Clan.

When the day of the auction came, no one could settle to work. It was being held too far away for any of them to attend, and Angus, although he had at first thought that he would go, changed his mind, feeling that ill news would travel fast enough, and he had no desire to know the worst. Instead he walked among the sheep, and drove up to the Castle, and walked the boundaries, watching for the deer, but the day was heavy and overcast, and they had hidden. He did not see a single beast. He noted that they had broken the fence in two places and that either he must mend it himself, or find a man who would do the jobs that Lexie had done for him, and then realised that this might no longer be his affair, and drove back to the cottage where he wandered aimlessly from kitchen to shed. He went to look at the ponies and found Grey standing forlorn, a triangular gash on his chest. He had been leaning over the barbed wire to graze beyond the fence and withdrawn his head carelessly.

Angus bathed the injury, and dressed it, and went inside the cottage again, to find that no more than half an hour had passed. He walked into the village, and paused at the post office, but no one had news. He walked on, towards the moorland at the other end of the loch.

Hooves sounded behind him, and, startled, he turned, and saw that the pony at Corrie Beg was loose on the road. The farmer came up, panting, and swore.

'Something upset him and he humped the wall. He has never done such a thing before,' the man said.

Angus watched the bay turn the corner of the road and vanish from sight. With any luck, he would keep straight on, so long as some car did not hoot at him or startle him, and he might be overtaken before he had gone too far. Pity that Grey was out of action. Bartie was nervous and hated traffic.

He went back and saddled the pony, and started off. The bay was still in sight when he rounded the bend, and began to trot along the straight narrow road that bordered the loch.

Bartie was glad to be out, to be free of the confines of the paddock, to have space ahead of him. It was easy to keep the bay in sight. The other pony stopped to graze, and then went on, curious, interested in everything about him, and quite unafraid.

The lorry that rounded the curve just before the enclosed moorland was not expecting to find a pony in the middle of the road. The driver swerved, tyres screaming, and the bay, terrified by the sudden unexpected apparition, leaped the fence and cantered over the rough grass towards the wood. Angus took Bartie into the fringe of trees that bordered the road and

138

waited until the lorry had passed, and then turned towards the moor.

There were only a few acres, belonging to the postmaster, rough ground, and woodland, and the blackened ruins of two old stone cottages. The villagers avoided it, and once some strangers from England had been permitted to put their caravan there for the night, when they had been unable to find another place to stay, and had left in the early morning, long before anyone was astir, anxious to get away. They did not know, then, why the moor was so alien and unwelcoming.

Angus knew. He knew that the bay pony would skirt the woodland copse, and stop on the other side, trembling with terror. He knew that Bartie would not go near the trees, that he must edge the field, careful to watch his way, and cross over the central part where the cottages gaped, roofless, at the sky. He did not care for the place himself and long ago, when he was a small boy, trespassing, he had wandered among the trees and felt the fear of the devil there, and been aware of eyes that watched from the leafy branches, and of creatures that stalked unseen behind him, yet, when he turned his head, the way was clear, and nothing troubled the space beyond him. He had never forgotten, and even now, over fifty years later, he was not sure that he cared to return.

The wind knifed from the water, and soughed in the branches and Bartie wanted to move sideways, away from it. He hated wind. He did not like the moor. His ears moved uneasily, and he stepped cautiously, ready to shy at the least movement, sure that other creatures besides himself lurked in the bushes and wished him ill.

Angus was close to the trees, and Bartie would not move, would not stir a foot, even though the man dismounted and pulled on the reins, coaxing him. At last he took the pony and tethered him to the fence, and walked along the edge of the wood, and found the bay standing, as he knew he would be, head hanging, drenched in sweat, trembling with fright.

Angus took him and haltered him, and led him away, and behind them the sky, which was dark with cloud, became the colour of sulphur, and glowed through the stark trees, and an eerie light fell on the little tarn, and Bartie tried to break away from the fence, and run.

Angus led the ponies out of the gate. He closed it, sighing with relief, ready to laugh at himself, yet unable to cast off the spell of the place.

Bartie sidestepped, and Angus came back to the present and the clouding sky and the fear that now the village must have new owners, and he would have to find another job. Black depression hit him without warning. He returned the bay to Corrie Beg, with only a curt word to the farmer, and took Bartie and unsaddled him and rubbed him down and fed both ponies, and then went to sit in the cottage, humped in the chair by the fire, the dogs lolling against him, until Andrew came and switched on the light, and announced that the Estate was sold, but that no one knew who the new owners might be, as an agent had bid for them. Rumour said they might come and live in the Castle, and that there would be big changes.

It was no kind of consolation at all, and Angus fetched the whisky bottle and poured a dram for both of them, and they were glooming together into the depths of their glasses when Jeannie came home, and after one look at the pair of them went out into the kitchen to cook a meal.

Chapter Sixteen

Two weeks later, Angus and Jeannie were sitting over a last cup
of tea at breakfast time when a large car drew up outside the
cottage.

'The new owners,' Angus said.

He did not want to open the door, did not wish to discover
who had bought up the Castle and the Estate, did not desire
to hear the news that they would be needing a younger man. He
opened the front door, his expression sour.

Ellen Gunn was waiting on the doorstep.

'Why, Angus, you look like the end of the world,' she said
in astonishment. 'Aren't you pleased to see me?'

'I thought it was someone else,' Angus said, feeling foolish,
as James Gunn walked up the front path and ducked his
head to enter the door.

'We had to come back. It was like coming home,' Ellen said.
She smiled at Jeannie. 'I thought you'd be married by now.'

Jeannie flushed.

'I've been too busy,' she said, defensively.

'That's always a mistake,' Ellen answered. 'Tell us, Angus,
what's been happening here since we went back to the States?'

'Too much, and none of it good,' Angus said. 'The Laird is
dead and strangers are coming to the Castle. And auld Lexie is
dead too, and there is little good that I can tell ye. We are
not happy about the new owners. Rumour says they will make
big changes, and that means that some of us will be looking for
work in other places.'

'Wouldn't you stay on if you liked the new owners, Angus?'

141

Ellen had lifted Kenzie on to her knee, and was stroking his soft fur. He looked up at her with oblique blue eyes and purred loudly

'He is a lovely cat. What do you call him?' she asked.

'Kenzie,' Jeannie said, and Kenzie acknowledged his name with a twitch of his ears.

'I can't see the new owners wanting an auld man, and a man who is lame at that,' Angus answered her first question, his expression dour. 'I broke my ankle and it will not heal enough to let me walk as far or as fast as I could before.'

'Perhaps the new owners will have their own ideas about that,' Ellen said, and her husband interrupted her suddenly.

'Don't tease, Ellen. It isn't fair. This is Angus's life and livelihood, and it means a great deal to him.'

'Angus, I'm so sorry. Only I wanted to surprise you.' Ellen looked up at him, repentant. 'You see, we have bought the Estate. We want to come and live in Scotland.'

'You have bought it?' Angus could only stare.

'I'm over sixty,' James Gunn said. 'I've worked hard all my life, and we thought it was time to rest. But retirement seemed so dull. We fell in love with Scotland. All our ancestors came from here originally and the place must be in our blood. When we heard from our son that the Castle was for sale, it seemed like an omen, and we decided to send an agent to bid for it. I had made plans to sell my own business and as soon as I heard that we had the Estate for certain, I put the plans into action.'

'What will ye do with the place?' Angus asked.

'That is why I'm worried about you, Angus. I don't know the Estate. Don't know its potentialities, or anything about it. I've lots of ideas, and the money to carry them out, but I need help to plan everything. I want to preserve the deer and re-stock part of the Dragon with capercaillie. Ellen and I have been reading about Scotland. We didn't think that you would ever want to leave here, Angus.'

Angus roused himself. He was umable to believe in such incredible fortune. All the old Laird's plans would be put into

142

effect, and the Gunns had the money to do it. Jeannie was as numbed as he, and stood, unable to say a word.

'I know it's not the same, Angus,' Ellen said gently. 'You must be very attached to the family. The yhave owned the Estate for so many years . . . for centuries. We're newcomers. So we'll need help. You will stay?'

'It is not that,' Angus said at last. 'We thought that strangers would come, people we did not know at all, people who would make changes and raise the rents, and kill the beasts, and sell off the village cottages, and perhaps the farm too. We did not expect that ye would ever come back. It's . . . well, it's a shock. But it is a very pleasant shock, and I will be very pleased to stay.'

'I've never heard you make such a long speech, Angus,' Ellen said, laughing. 'Jeannie, can we have a cup of tea to celebrate? I'll have to get used to tea in Scotland, now we are going to live here. I'm so excited . . . and our son is getting married to a Scottish girl and not going back to America, so we'll be able to be near him. And we have so many friends over here . . .'

'I'll want to spend several days with you, Angus, and have you take me round the Estate,' James Gunn said. 'And I want to buy a fishing rod, and you can teach me how to fish for trout and salmon. And I want to breed sheep. I've always wanted sheep. A pedigree flock. And cattle. I've often dreamed of living like this but I never thought it would come true.'

Jeannie poured the tea, and later took Ellen to see Rusty and the hind, and to greet the two ponies, and to look out over the loch, where a seal was rolling, his back showing sleek and black and shining against the blue water that reflected a sky humped with tiny white clouds that were massing above the mountain. Ellen watched the waves break on the rocks, and looked up at the Dragon, which lay quiet under the sun.

'It's so peaceful here,' she said. 'No hurry or rush or bustle. There's so much to do, too. We don't want to alter the Castle. We want to leave it as it is, except that we are going to put central heating in, and to furnish the little housekeeper's room as a small sitting-room where we can be cosy. I feel as if I belong already. I think it was the piper, Donald Gunn, who made me want to come here to live. And Lexie. I'm sorry about Lexie.'

'He was trying to rescue Rusty,' Jeannie said.

Life was suddenly brighter. Her father would not lose his job, and would find new interest in helping build up the Estate. He often talked of the old days, and the money that had been lavished on the place before death duties became so crippling. It would mean all kinds of changes, but all of them good. The place would be properly managed again, the fences and walls repaired, and perhaps her father would have a better home, on the Dragon, nearer to his work. The sheep would have good grazing.

James Gunn believed in getting things done and getting them done swiftly, even in the north-west where tomorrow was as good as today and the day after that much better. He brought men to install an oil-fired furnace and central heating, and ground, just out of sight of the Castle, was marked out, and levelled, and builders' lorries moved in. Angus saw them drive through the far entrance behind the Castle, and went to look. James Gunn joined him.

'That's where you'll live,' he said, pointing to the cleared site. 'You're much too far from your work down there in the village. And your sheep are on rotten pasture. Bring them back here, and let them graze in the field. The grass is good, and there's food for yours and mine as well.'

'Mine are some of the old Laird's breeding,' Angus said. 'He let me have them cheap when he sold off the flock. They're pure bred and good stock, and ye cannot do better. If ye would like to buy the ewe lambs next year . . .'

By lambing time Angus was installed in the new house. Jeannie could not get used to such luxury. She spent hours admiring the astonishing fittings in the kitchen and bathroom, and showed Andrew round with pride when he came. He looked at her uneasily. After such a palace she would never settle down in the kind of home that he could afford. He was curt when she spoke to him, and she was annoyed, thinking that he was uninterested. Davie Grey was visiting again, having come to

144

interview the new owner of the Castle and to write an article about his plans to improve the Estate. He was much more receptive, and praised everything that she showed him.

The animals had settled well. Bartie and Grey had a paddock to run in and when the weather was at its worst, could be housed in the stables belonging to the Castle, which were close to Angus's new home. There were shelters for the two deer. Rusty was now a very large beast, but he was as affectionate as ever. He had not lost his antlers after he had been gelded which surprised everyone, including the Vet. They were not branched, but would be single points like his first growth, so he did not look too strange.

Jeannie was restless. She was too far away from the village to help with the school, although she went three times a week to see the old ladies. Angus drove her down when he went to the store, and fetched her back at night. She wanted to return to the hospital, but the doctor was sure that her leg would not stand the strain of long hours on duty and so much running about.

'If you did it part time, it would be all right,' he said at last, and Jeannie considered the idea. She felt that she had no right to let her father keep her, even though James Gunn had increased his salary, saying that he was now much more of an estate manager than a gamekeeper. There were Aberdeen Angus cattle in the big field behind the Castle, and sheep on the hill, and Highland cattle on the rough ground at the side of the loch. Angus had plenty to interest him. James Gunn was fascinated by the intricacies of farming the Estate, and cutting off part of the hill to make a sanctuary for the deer. They could leap the fences, but at least the hinds would be safe when they calved, and he wanted to use more of the ground, and make jump-proof enclosures. There was so much to do.

Angus spent less and less time at home, and Jeannie became even more restive, so that when Davie proposed to her, and suggested that she could go back to nursing when they were married, she accepted him. She showed Angus her ring, a pretty thing, sapphires and diamonds set in a circle, and he admired it, but wondered privately if she had chosen the right man. He could not imagine her living away from animals. And Davie did not care even for the cat. He wondered what Kenzie would do in a flat in Glasgow, and whether Jeannie would take the little beast when she went. There would be problems there.

Andrew no longer came to see her, although he and Angus often met and talked about the forest and the deer, and the prospects of fishing, and Andrew was always ready to help with the management of the Estate, and fascinated by the progress that James Gunn made daily. Each week showed new improvements.

Andrew came to see the piggery.

'Lexie would have revelled in this,' Angus said, as he watched the sow nosing her swill in the brand new pen. Every modern facility for pig keeping surrounded her. She grunted and stretched herself in a patch of sunlight and went to sleep.

'When is Jeannie getting wed?' Andrew asked. He wanted to know the date, to know when she would be away. It would be easier after she had gone. While she stayed he saw her daily, walking down the hill, playing with the two deer, and the dogs, and Kenzie came to greet him, as if wondering why he no longer came to the house. When she had gone for good, he could forget her. Forget the way she walked, the way she looked up at him, the shape of her lips when she smiled, the wide cat eyes that were so calm and so unrevealing as she went about her work.

'She will not make up her mind,' Angus said. 'Not for six months at least, she says. She wants time to prepare her trousseau, and they have to find a flat, and Davie is not always free. His editor keeps him busy and with a wife to provide for, he will be busier than ever. She says she will work in the hospital again.'

It was little consolation. Andrew wished that the next few months were gone, and that he ran no risk of seeing her when he had to pass the house. He drove by daily on his way to his own work. He often paused to watch Rusty, who was now full grown, a handsome animal, with all the elegance of

146

his kind, his head turning to gaze mild-eyed, at those who came near the paddock. Angus had made a high fence to keep him safe. Neither he nor the hind had any wild-sense, and neither was protected by terror of man. James Gunn had suggested the high fences, knowing how Jeannie felt about her animals.

Jeannie passed through the days in a dream, thinking of her wedding, and of the clothes she would buy, and the way she would furnish the flat. Sometimes Davie wondered if he was real to her, as she was abstracted when he came, and she did not respond to his eagerness, remaining as aloof as if they were not engaged.

'Time enough when we are wed,' she told him, and he had to be content, although it annoyed him more and more to see the fuss she made of the cat or the way she greeted the two deer, who waited for her by the gate, anxious for attention.

Rusty loved to nuzzle against her neck, and thrust a greedy nose into the basket she carried, or into her pocket looking for titbits. He was always delighted to see her, and when she had been out of the house, and came back past his field, he galloped to meet her, and protested loudly if she failed to come and stroke him.

'I cannot think what he will do when I have gone,' she said one morning, and Angus glanced at her sharply. She seemed less anxious to leave home, but perhaps it was always like that. It was a big change for a lass, wedding a man who must be almost a stranger, as there were so many things about him that she could not know. And Davie was becoming morose. He had thought that she would be more affectionate when they were engaged, but she seemed much less so, and he snapped at her when she picked up the cat, or went to feed the beasts.

'It will be easier when she's married,' Ellen said, coming over to the house one day with patterns of wedding dresses, cut from a magazine. 'It's a trying time for a girl, and it will be a big change for Jeannie. She's spent most of her life here, and she did not care for Glasgow when she was there before. She told me it was too big, all shops and houses and hurrying people, and she knew so few of them. It's friendly

147

on the Dragon, and we know everyone in the village and they know us. I already feel as if I belong.'

Ellen had busied herself joining the Women's Institute, bringing American recipes to liven up the meetings, so that many husbands found themselves enjoying Chicken Maryland, and eating other dishes with unusual names and even more unusual mixtures of food. Not all were sure that they liked the new dishes, but the women were enthusiastic. Variety in their cooking added interest to an occupation that often palled, so that many of them wished there were other meats to cook, or other vegetables to try.

'You see, it will be all right,' Ellen insisted. 'I'll help her with her clothes, and with the arrangements, and before you know where you are you'll be a grandfather. Nelson wrote today to say that his Mary is going to have a bairn in seven months' time. It seems no time at all since the wedding, and yet that was almost six months ago now.'

Angus congratulated her, and was comforted. Perhaps by this time next year he too would have the knowledge that Jeannie was going to have a bairn. He whistled as he walked to the Land-Rover. He wanted to find catalogues and order an incubator for the grouse chicks. No more improvising. He saw Andrew and waved, and then sighed, as the forester nodded curtly and walked away. Jeannie was coming up the hill and he did not wish to meet her. Life was never simple, Angus thought, as he climbed into the Land-Rover. He passed Andrew farther down the drive.

'Would ye like a lift to the village?' he asked, but Andrew shook his head. He would have to move, and he had asked for a transfer. If only Jeannie would marry Davie soon and go away. The forester did not want to leave the Nine Glens. He enjoyed his work and he loved the Dragon, and knew every mood and every variation, from winter snowfall, through the spring greening to midsummer brightness and autumn haze. He had always lived within sight of the loch and the mountains and he hated change.

Chapter Seventeen

By the time that the stags roared their challenge on the mountains Jeannie had agreed to fix a date for the wedding. Davie was busy, and only able to visit her rarely, but when he came he brought gifts with him; nylon pillowcases, gay towels, a pottery vase, all of which she put away in her room, ready to use when they were married.

The sky glowered above the Dragon, grey and dark with rain, day after day. The wind savaged the trees, battering and blustering, tearing down branches, rending one giant elm, which grew beside the road along the loch edge, from the ground, so that a team of men had to come and work on it and shift it. The road was blocked for several hours.

Rusty and the hind grazed in the paddock. Jeannie wondered if one of the stags might scent her and come looking for her, but none came near, and the two beasts were company for one another. Fly often came to see her one-time fosterling, and if he were too bold and chased and teased her, she snapped at him angrily and he withdrew meekly.

One Sunday afternoon, a youth called Jack Melton was walking on the Dragon. He had saved every penny for months to buy himself a gun, and now he had it. It was the best that he could afford, and he handled it lovingly. The shining barrel and the gleaming stock gave him great satisfaction, and he practised, day after day, until he was sure of hitting the target dead centre. He knew just how to hold the gun, how to sight, and he had telescopic sights to ensure perfect aim. He lay with the butt against his shoulder, and breathed in deeply, and released his breath slowly and squeezed the trigger gently and watched the marks on the target until success was guaranteed.

He had never lived in the country. He came from a high flat in a factory town, and he did not know that he needed a licence for the gun, which he had bought from a man he met at work.

He did not know that he could not shoot deer whenever or wherever he chose, or that the Dragon was now a sanctuary. He did know that he must be quiet, he must be cunning, and he must be cautious, or he would not be able to get near enough to kill a deer. He knew that he must watch the wind, and that he must not step on a twig, or he would alarm his quarry. He did not know where the deer hid, but he did know that when he had walked on the Dragon some weeks before he had seen two in a clearing among the trees.

He climbed swiftly, eager to try his skill. He did not notice the clouds that hung over the mountains, or the wind that ripped the wave tops, not the sigh of the waves below him, or the noise of the swaying trees. He did not hear the roar from the corrie above him as the Master challenged a small beast and drove him away, and herded the hinds even higher on the hill. He did not see the birds that watched him and that called a warning that the roaming deer heeded, so that they vanished, silent as dawn.

Jeannie heard the bird calls, and knew there was danger on the mountain. She did not know where. She looked anxiously lest a prowling fox was near the hen run, or a stray dog running among the sheep. Nothing moved. The sheep were untroubled, feeding quietly, the cattle stood lazily, tails swinging, and Rusty and the hind stood together near the gate, watching her as she moved about the garden, hanging clothes up on the line.

Angus and James Gunn were standing by the new pig sties, discussing one of the sows, and making plans for the Aberdeen Angus herd. James Gunn wanted to immerse himself in the life of the country, to breed pedigree beasts and show them and win awards. He had his eye on several coveted prizes. He was finding a satisfaction in this new way of life that had never been there in the old days. Animals were rewarding. One of the cows already knew him and greeted him with a rub of her head against his shoulder whenever he came near her, and Angus was training a retriever for him, a beautiful golden dog called Major, who followed at heel and thought James Gunn the most wonderful man in the world. He was sitting beside his master now, and the American stooped and caressed the long silky ears and was rewarded with an effusive lick and a frantic tail. Mac watched quietly, knowing that Angus was training the other dog and that he must be accepted.

It was almost dinner time. Jeannie had cooked a special meal, as Davie was coming, and she could already hear the sound of his engine as he drove up the road leading to the Castle, and the house that stood in the grounds behind it. Perhaps that was what had alerted the birds. Their calls were more urgent now, and she looked for Kenzie, but he was stretched in the sun on the sill inside the dining-room window, and offered no harm to any of them.

She watched Rusty amble across the paddock, the hind trotting behind him, always a faithful shadow. He was a splendid beast, over two years old, and within a year or so he would be even bigger as none of his strength would go into producing calves. She wondered if he still missed the herd, and she whistled to him, and he saw her and turned his head, and bounded towards her, every movement graceful.

The youth on the hill saw nothing but the bounding deer. He did not hear the girl call, nor see the men beyond him. He drew in his breath. Here was glory. Here was the culminating point of the long months of saving for the gun, for the feel of power in his hands, the ability to kill, the ultimate climax of destruction.

He squeezed the trigger. Jeannie saw the deer fall, saw blood pour from the massive neck artery, saw his eyes glaze and his legs kick, and his head, in that last moment, turn towards her, his eyes looking for her. She flung open the gate and ran inside, screaming, scarcely aware that she had heard the shot as the beast fell. The youth, startled, moved incautiously, and she heard him. Rusty was beyond all help, and died as she knelt beside him. Davie, bringing his car to a stop, saw the youth hesitating, his face uncertain. He had had no idea that anyone would ever keep a tame deer.

Jeannie stood up. She saw Jack outside the paddock and saw his gun. She walked towards him. He stared at her, horrified.

Her face was white, and her dress was soaked in blood from the beast that he had killed. He did not know what to say, nor what to do, and was quite unprepared for the sudden attack that she launched on him, tearing the gun away from him, hitting him in fury, pummelling at his face and his shoulders, until Davie came running and pulled her away, saying 'For God's sake, Jeannie.'

Angus and James raced towards them. Both men were furious, and James found it hard to keep his temper. He had been fond of Rusty, and the deer had learned to know him in the past few months, and he knew too how Jeannie had fought to save the deer from death, not once, but several times, nursing him through the first days of his life in captivity and through several illnesses, bringing him back to health after the dog had savaged him in his brief days of freedom.

The hind stood beside her dead companion, her eyes puzzled.

'Guard him, Mac,' Angus said, and the dog bared his teeth, and Jack wished he had never left his home, never heard of guns, never come to this place, never set eyes on the deer. He swallowed.

'You had better get the police, Angus,' James Gunn said. 'I'll take this mighty hunter, this killer of pet deer, to the Castle.'

He took hold of the lad's collar but Jack had no urge to resist. His brief triumph was forgotten. It had been a perfect shot. He would never shoot any living creature again, as long as he lived. He had never thought beyond the instant of death, to the dying beast, and the spilling blood, and the bellow of pain as it was hit, or imagined anything like the scream of the girl who had run towards it. He began to shake. Mac was following him, ready to bite at the least sign of panic, of running away, and the man who towered above him, grim-faced, was

152

even more frightening than the girl or the dog. He began to feel that life was most unfair.

Jeannie stood at the gate, and looked at the dead deer. Everything that she loved was taken from her. The hind came to her, and pushed at her hand, and she fondled the soft ears. She did not want anyone near her, least of all Davie, who irritated her immensely by standing beside her, unable to find words.

'It's best that way,' he said at last. 'He would have missed you when you came to Glasgow.'

Jeannie looked up at him.

'I'm not coming to Glasgow,' she said. 'It's no use, Davie. I can't leave the Dragon. This has made me certain. I can't take Kenzie into a flat. I can't live among houses and shops. I belong here.'

She took off her ring, and gave it to him, and walked away. He stared after her, his face forlorn. Angus said nothing. There was nothing he could say. He watched his daughter go indoors and lift the cat from the windowsill, and carry him out of the room. He heard her climb the stairs, heard her bedroom door shut, heard the key turn in the lock.

'We had better bury the deer, and then have our dinner,' he said.

Davie turned away.

'I'll be going. It is no use staying here now. Tell Jeannie she can keep the things I bought her. I don't want them.'

Angus watched him drive away. He telephoned to the village policeman, and then went to look at the deer. No use letting Rusty go for venison. Not even he could bear the thought, and he was still looking down at the dead beast when Andrew arrived in his Land-Rover.

'I heard that Jeannie was shot,' he said. His dark eyes looked anxiously at Angus.

'She is not shot,' Angus said. Andrew came and stood beside him and looked down at Rusty. He had no words either. He helped the keeper dig a grave, and helped bury the deer, remembering how often he had watched the bounding beauty of the beast as he played in the paddock, and stroked the

153

dark fur, and in past days watched Jeannie feed the calf from the bottle.

He was aware of her as they filled in the last spadefuls of earth on the raw grave. She was watching from under the trees. He forgot that she was engaged to Davie. He forgot that he had no right to comfort her. He walked across to her and looked down at her with a gentle expression in his eyes.

'I mind too, Jeannie,' he said.

She was against his coat, crying as if she would never stop. His arms were tight around her, his lips were against her hair. When Kenzie came wailing, jealous, he held out his arm and the little cat jumped on to it, and climbed on to Jeannie's shoulder, purring.

'You can have more beasts, Jeannie,' he said. 'There is aye room for another. There will always be deer on the hill. You will have to learn . . . not even Kenzie can live for ever. Each creature has his place. And ye will never forget Rusty.'

It was hard not to sorrow, but Jeannie went to bed comforted. Andrew knew that Davie had gone, and he knew that in time Jeannie would come to him. He lay watching the moon that night, and thinking of her, and of the dead deer, and all that it had meant to her. It was such a futile, stupid kind of death. It was hours before he slept.

Jeannie, in her own room heard the stags calling. The little hind had been fretting, searching the paddock for Rusty, and Angus had brought her close to the house, where she stood with the ponies, all three dark shapes in the moonlight.

Jeannie looked out of the window. The Dragon was serene, no sound of wind, no sign of movement, and the moon rode high in the sky, gilding the loch. On the hillside above her the stags roared in anger, and raged at each other, and fought and fled, or fought and conquered. It was a life that Rusty could never have known.

Below her, the loch glinted. A small wind rushed up the hillside and the shadows moved. There was a fourth beast in the orchard. She looked out, startled, and saw a stag there, nosing the hind. He was no older than Rusty and his antlers showed

154

white on his head. The hind nuzzled against him. She was too young to breed, and so, in all probability, was he, but the herd had no time for him, and he was lonely. Perhaps next year he would come back again and the hind would calve, and there would be another deer to care for, this time a calf with his own mother to guard him.

By morning the young stag had gone.

Jeannie made breakfast, and fed the ponies. The wind blustered over the loch. Rusty's grave was a bitter reminder. She took flowers and put them on it, remembering how she had done this for her dog, long ago. She was looking down at the shining petals when Andrew arrived, carrying a foal in his arms.

'His mother is dead, and I said that ye would care for him. He will grow into a grand wee beast.'

Angus glanced at the forester, wondering where in the world he had found the foal, half guessing that Andrew had got up early that morning and phoned every vet in the directory. The foal was providential. Jeannie would be busy caring for the little creature, and would not have time for grief.

'She'll never change,' he said, as he watched her take a bottle of milk and coax the orphan to feed.

'I would not want her to.'

Andrew went outside, and sat on the wall beside her, as she bent over the foal. She looked up at him, and suddenly she knew that he was right for her, that whatever she did, he would find no fault. He shared her concern for the animals about them, and would help her to look after them whenever he got the chance.

The foal sucked at her finger, and Jeannie turned to him. He was impatient for food, and completely trusting. She stroked his neck, and her eyes clouded, and in that moment she saw again the gentle face and brown eyes of the deer calf, his dark fur, dappled with white, the twitching ears, and the way he moved his head.

Up on the hill the Master roared in challenge and the wind swept the Dragon, and raked the Nine Glens and excitement rode on the mountain. Rusty had gone but there would be new calves in the spring. Kenzie came to look at the foal, and to rub against his mistress and to remind her that he was there. He would never allow her to forget him. She gentled his fur, and he rolled on his back and bit her hand in play.

Ellen Gunn, coming to see the foal, saw Jeannie and Andrew together, and smiled.

'Are you happy now, Angus?' she asked.

'Aye,' Angus answered.

He was never a man for words.

ZARA by JOYCE STRANGER

Richard Proud coveted the golden-brown mare from the moment he saw her. Although he couldn't afford Zara, he bought her nevertheless, to breed him winners – foals that would restore the fortune of the Yorkshire stud where he bred and trained racehorses.

Zara was born a winner. She had to be raced and Richard Proud was determined that she should race; so despite personal crises – caused by his reckless wife – a snowstorm that isolated the stud only a few days before Zara was due to run, and an accident to her jockey, he had to find a way to let Zara prove her ability ...

'Mrs Stranger's understanding of animals is sane and unsentimental, and her picture of the racing community is satisfying.' – *Oxford Mail*

0 552 09892 – £1.50

THE MONASTERY CAT AND OTHER ANIMALS
by JOYCE STRANGER

Here, from Joyce Stranger, Britain's best-loved writer of animal stories, are all the animals that she understands and describes so well ... pedigree cats and barnyard strays, working dogs and family pets, wild horses and untamed animals from the sea and the jungle ...

Joyce Stranger can write about animals as no other writer – and make you love them ...

SBN 0 552 12044 8 – £1.50

BREED OF GIANTS by JOYCE STRANGER

Few of those who have seen the Shire Personality of the Year, standing splendid in the spotlight at the Horse of the Year Show, dwarfing the herald's more delicate mounts, will ever forget the giant horse – proud and handsome, head held high, mane brilliant with tiny standards, tail braided with ribbons.

This book tells the story of Josh Johnson, a farmer, who breeds his gigantic Shire horses and, with fanatical devotion, brings them up to championship status, only to have his hopes shattered by an accident to his best horse and an outbreak of foot-and-mouth disease on a neighbouring farm.

How Josh copes with his burdens and builds once more his winning strain of Shires, is told with all Joyce Stranger's skill and charm.

0 552 09893 0 – 85p

KYM by JOYCE STRANGER

Joyce Stranger's novels have become well-loved favourites with all age groups. Her first non-fiction book is sure to take its place among them.

Kym is the autobiography of her Siamese cat who, for thirteen years, adored her, dominated her, and played havoc with her life. A more accident-prone cat never lived. Even on holiday he managed to turn their caravan into an ambulance – or a peep-show. A born eccentric and voluble talker, a cat with the grace of a dancer and the instincts of a prizefighter.

An endearing story of the misadventures of a unique pet, seen through Kym's blue-eyed squint, and his owner's humorous and observant eyes.

0 552 10695 X – £1.50

A SELECTED LIST OF CORGI BOOKS

WHILE EVERY EFFORT IS MADE TO KEEP PRICES LOW, IT IS SOMETIMES NECESSARY TO INCREASE PRICES AT SHORT NOTICE. CORGI BOOKS RESERVE THE RIGHT TO SHOW AND CHARGE NEW RETAIL PRICES ON COVERS WHICH MAY DIFFER FROM THOSE ADVERTISED IN THE TEXT OR ELSEWHERE.

THE PRICES SHOWN BELOW WERE CORRECT AT THE TIME OF GOING TO PRESS (NOVEMBER '82).

☐	11993 8	UP TO SCRATCH	*Diana Cooper*	£1.50
☐	11364 6	ANIMAL HOTEL	*Diana Cooper*	£1.50
☐	12014 6	ANY FOOL CAN BE A DAIRY FARMER	*James Robertson*	£1.50
☐	10127 3	ONE FOR SORROW	*Joyce Stranger*	85p
☐	11951 2	THREE'S A PACK	*Joyce Stranger*	1.50
☐	09893 0	BREED OF GIANTS	*Joyce Stranger*	85p
☐	09462 5	LAKELAND VET	*Joyce Stranger*	70p
☐	11803 6	HOW TO OWN A SENSIBLE DOG	*Joyce Stranger*	1.25
☐	12044 8	THE MONASTERY CAT AND OTHER ANIMALS	*Joyce Stranger*	1.50
☐	10125 7	CASEY	*Joyce Stranger*	1.50
☐	09892 2	ZARA	*Joyce Stranger*	1.50
☐	10685 2	FLASH	*Joyce Stranger*	1.50
☐	10311 X	REX	*Joyce Stranger*	1.50
☐	10695 X	KYM	*Joyce Stranger*	1.50

All these books are available at your local book shop or newsagent, or can be ordered direct from the publisher. Just tick the titles you want and fill in the form below.

CORGI BOOKS, Cash Sales Department, P.O. Box 11, Falmouth, Cornwall.

Please send cheque or postal order, no currency.

Please allow cost of book(s) plus the following for postage and packing:

U.K. Customers – Allow 45p for the first book, 20p for the second book and 14p for each additional book ordered, to a maximum charge of £1.63.

B.F.P.O. and Eire – Allow 45p for the first book, 20p for the second book plus 14p per copy for the next 7 books, thereafter 8p per book.

Overseas Customers – Allow 75p for the first book and 21p per copy for each additional book.

NAME (Block Letters) ....

ADDRESS ....

....